*A
Harlequin
Romance*

OTHER
Harlequin Romances
by JANICE GRAY

1167—DEAR BARBARIAN
1230—CROWN OF CONTENT
1275—SHAKE OUT THE STARS
1707—GARDEN OF THE SUN

WINTER LOVING

by

JANICE GRAY

HARLEQUIN BOOKS   TORONTO
WINNIPEG

Original hard cover edition published in 1973
by Mills & Boon Limited.

© Janice Gray 1973

SBN 373-01744-8

Harlequin edition published December 1973

Printed in Canada

1744

CHAPTER I

Fiona had dreamt about coming home to Inveray so many times that now it was actually happening she found she could hardly believe it.

It was dusk, so that although she pressed her face eagerly against the car window she could only just see the outlines of the towering mountains on either side of the narrow road. Not that it really mattered. She knew they wouldn't have changed. Mountains didn't. Only people.

'Ye've no' forgot the way, Miss Fiona?' The man behind the steering wheel spoke gruffly, without turning his grizzled head.

'No, Angus, I've not forgotten.' Fiona smiled as she answered him. Some people didn't change, either. It was eight years since she had last seen Angus, and yet he was just as she remembered him—dour, silent, undemonstrative. However glad he was to see her back, he'd never ever say so. Though of course if Neil had been with her . . .

Fiona smiled and glanced at her small daughter, curled up beside her on the back seat. Jenny's pale gold head was drooping, her dark-fringed eyes heavy with fatigue. America to Scotland was a long and tiring journey for a seven-year-old, Fiona thought with a pang of compunction. Not, of course, that Jenny, American born and bred, had been anything but wildly excited at the prospect of a holiday in the Highlands, where her mother had lived before her marriage to Neil Campbell. She'd wanted to know all about the rivers and burns and hills and—most of all—about the old grey-walled house where her grandparents lived.

5

Cragside, huge and bleak, standing out against the dark pine woods that clothed the hills behind it. . . .

There had been Campbells at Cragside for generations. Her husband, Neil, used to joke about it. 'Don't forget I'm the last of the line so that I'm expected to produce about half a dozen sons!' he'd told Fiona shortly after their marriage. Then, laughing, 'But you needn't worry, darling. I'm not greedy. I'll settle for half that number!'

Only there were to be no sons at all for Neil. He had been killed in a car accident only six weeks before his first child was born. The child who had proved to be a daughter, a tiny replica of her mother with the same golden hair and clear grey eyes.

Jenny stirred and yawned. 'Are we nearly there, Mommy?'

What would the Campbells think of their granddaughter's American accent? Fiona wondered ruefully. Aloud she said, 'I think we must be, darling. I'm not quite sure.'

'Granny and Grandpapa will be pleased to see us, won't they?'

Fiona put her arm round the child's slight body, hugging her close.

'Of course they will! Didn't I read you what Granny said in her letter? She wants to see us very badly. That's why we're here.'

It had been a fine sunny day in Miami when Margaret Campbell's letter had arrived. Fiona had known, directly she picked it up, who it was from, though it wasn't the writing—small and neat—that had given her the clue. It was the postmark.

For a few moments she had stood quite still, turning the envelope over in her hands. It was absurd the way her throat had suddenly tightened. Absurd that even now, after eight years, she hadn't been able to discipline herself to forget the things that were better forgotten!

Upstairs, Jenny was singing. For a seven-year-old she had an astounding knowledge of the latest 'pop' tunes, Fiona thought ruefully as she tore open the envelope and drew out a single sheet of notepaper. Her mother-in-law, always busy with some activity or another, rarely had time to write at length and her infrequent letters were usually no more than a brief, dutiful 'keeping in touch.' This one, though, was different. As Fiona's eye travelled down the page the sense of what she was reading dropped into her consciousness like little drops of ice.

Douglas Campbell, Margaret's husband and Fiona's father-in-law, was going slowly blind and within six months would probably lose his sight altogether. Margaret wrote in unemotional, factual phrases that Fiona knew must mask a breaking heart.

It wasn't until the end of her letter that Margaret allowed her grief to show. 'Please, Fiona, won't you consider coming home for a month or two so that we can see and get to know our only grandchild? I am sure that this would give Douglas the greatest possible joy as he so often talks about her these days and says how much he wishes that you hadn't decided to stay in America after poor Neil's death. . . .' And, finally, 'We would be only too happy to send the money for your fares and any other expenses. Douglas has made one or two lucky investments lately and money really is no problem. Please do, do think our proposal over very carefully and say "Yes", chiefly for our sake but for Jenny's too. After all, she has never been to Scotland, and yet you and Neil were always so proud of your Scottish heritage. . . .'

Recalling those words as the speeding car brought them nearer and nearer to Inveray, Fiona felt her eyes pricking with sudden tears. Perhaps she had been wrong . . . selfish . . . to stay on in America after Neil's death. Perhaps he would have wanted her to return to Scotland with his child. Nobody had been able to understand her decision to remain where she was, for even though her father, who had been the Presbyterian minister at Inveray, was dead it was taken for granted that she knew that there would always be a place for her in that small, close-knit community. And Jenny, after all, was the Laird's granddaughter.

Jenny's small hand tugged insistently at her arm. 'Tell me about Inveray again, Mommy! Will I see the house where you were born?'

'I expect so,' Fiona said, smiling.

'And the places where you used to play? Will you show me the loch where you and Daddy used to go fishing and where you once fell in?'

Fiona looked at her daughter in amusement. 'I must have told you about that ages ago! Fancy you remembering!'

'You didn't tell me everything. Who pulled you out? Was it Daddy?'

There was a moment's silence. Then Fiona said, as naturally as she could, 'No. No, it wasn't Daddy.'

'Then who was it?'

Fiona hesitated, conscious that Angus, in the front seat, must be listening to every word. Then she said briefly, 'Somebody else Daddy and I used to play with. His name was Rowan. He was the doctor's son.'

'Did he have to life-save you?' Jenny asked breathlessly.

'Well, not exactly. But I couldn't swim at that

8

time and I doubt if I could have reached the bank by myself.'

She was glad she didn't have to tell Jenny that Neil, always a little slower to react than his friend, had been merely an onlooker. Not, of course, that his help had been needed. Rowan had had the situation well in hand. The eldest of the three, he was their acknowledged leader. Wherever he went, Fiona and Neil had followed, eagerly, unquestioningly. For a few years the three of them, Laird's son, doctor's son and minister's daughter, had enjoyed an almost perfect comradeship. Then Rowan had gone away to university and Neil had followed him, and somehow, during their vacations, things had never been quite the same.

Jenny snuggled up against her mother's shoulder and Fiona closed her eyes, remembering. It came almost as a shock when she heard Angus's gruff voice announcing that they had arrived at Inveray.

They turned into a narrow, bumpy lane which wound steeply upwards. They were among the trees: tall Scotch pines grew all around and the pointed peak of Ben Leithen Dui rose clear-cut against the dusky sky. The high banks were thick with bracken, the road filled with shadows. Fiona drew a long breath. There was the heavy, wrought-iron gate she remembered so well. There was the name, almost indiscernible in the fading light: Cragside.

Jenny clutched her mother's hand as the car edged its way slowly up a long, pebbly drive. 'Goodness, isn't it big!' she whispered as the house, built of stone, with a square tower and long straight windows, came into view. 'It's almost like a castle!'

Margaret Campbell must have been waiting for them close at hand, for Angus had barely touched the horn before the massive front door was flung open and light streamed out. Margaret, thin and angular, her brown hair liberally streaked with grey and looking much older than when Fiona had last seen her, came hurrying to meet them. Fiona held out her hands. Margaret took them and stood looking at her daughter-in-law and the child by her side in silence. Then ' Welcome home!' she said softly, and bent to kiss Jenny's cheek.

Douglas Campbell was waiting for them in the great hall, leaning heavily on a stick. He welcomed Fiona and Jenny as warmly as his wife had done, his eyes lingering on his granddaughter as if trying to find in her some resemblance to the dead son he had adored.

' My dear, it's good to see you both! I can't tell you how happy we are that you decided to come.' Douglas Campbell's face looked tired and grey and his eyes were shielded by dark glasses, but his voice was still strong and firm. He smiled at Jenny as he added, ' And now that you're here we hope that you're going to stay for a long, long time.'

Jenny liked the look of her grandfather. Fiona could tell that by the way she smiled and nodded her head. Almost immediately afterwards, however, she gave a huge yawn and her grandmother laughed sympathetically.

' She's tired, poor bairn. What about supper and bed for her straightaway, Fiona? We can have our meal after she's settled down.'

Jenny protested, but only half-heartedly. Worn out by excitement and the long journey, she was almost asleep on her feet.

' You've tomorrow and all the days after tomorrow to explore the house and get to know Granny and Grandpapa,' Fiona told her. ' Come on, sleepy-head, let's get you to bed.'

'I don't want anything to eat. Just some hot chocolate, please.'

'Right. I'll see to that in a minute,' Margaret said.

Jenny looked at her grandfather. 'Goodnight, Grandpapa.'

'Goodnight, lassie. Sleep well.' He bent down to kiss her forehead, then she and Fiona followed Margaret up the spiral staircase and along a wide passage where stout oak doors opened on either side. Margaret opened the second door along and showed Jenny a small bedroom with rose-patterned walls and pink curtains.

'Your mother's bedroom is just next door, Jenny. That door there leads into it, so you won't feel lonely, will you?'

Margaret Campbell's rather severe features softened into a smile as she addressed her granddaughter. 'She approves of her,' Fiona thought, and was conscious of a rush of relief.

Jenny shook her head and stood gazing around her with wide grey eyes.

'Like it?' Fiona asked, sure that she did.

'Mmmm. Where's the bathroom?'

'Just down the corridor, if my memory serves me right.' Fiona turned away and bent over the suitcase containing Jenny's pyjamas, flannel and toothbrush. By the time the child was in bed Margaret had arrived with a mug of hot chocolate and Jenny sipped it sitting propped up against her pillows.

Margaret moved towards the door. 'We'll see you downstairs in a few minutes' time, Fiona. I expect you'd like to wash and change before dinner.'

'Thank you. I won't be long.' Fiona tucked Jenny up, kissed her goodnight and went into the adjoining

11

bedroom to make a hurried toilet. The walls were rose-patterned, like Jenny's, but the curtains were chintz and the carpet a soft dove-grey. There was a photograph of Neil on the dressing table.

Fiona hesitated, then picked it up, staring down at the smiling face. Her own was sombre. Neil must have been about twenty when this was taken. Two years later he was married and on his way to America, a country which for him had always held an almost uncanny fascination. Fiona had often heard him, as a boy, talk about his ambitions to settle in Florida or California. Only she'd laughed at him then ... refused to take him seriously.

' How can you possibly want to live anywhere else but Scotland?' she'd demanded, waving her hand at the tree-covered hills which rose into mountains, bare and craggy and heather-clad. She'd certainly never thought, in those days, that one day she'd be only too glad to make America her permanent home. That marriage to Neil would offer her an escape from an unhappiness almost too great to bear.

Somewhere, a door slammed. The noise jerked Fiona out of her painful thoughts and back to the present. She put the photograph down with a little sigh. Poor Neil! He'd been so young, so full of life. And so determined to have his own way, whatever the cost. He'd known, when he married her, that she wasn't in love with him. She'd been absolutely honest about that. But it hadn't mattered—or he'd said it didn't matter. Then. It was only after their marriage that he'd become difficult and demanding. Fiona had tried hard to be the kind of wife he wanted, but nothing she ever said or did really satisfied him. His fierce, unreasonable jealousy had been the cause of frequent quarrels—ugly, bitter quarrels which had left

Fiona feeling heartsick and defeated. Perhaps things would have been different after Jenny's birth. Perhaps . . . but she'd never know.

She changed into a soft blue woollen dress which did subtle things for her delicate colouring and gave her honey-gold hair, which hung to her shoulders, a hard brushing. A dusting of powder . . . a dash of lipstick . . . and she was ready.

Jenny was already asleep, her bright head pillowed on her arms. Fiona stood looking down at her, her lips curving into a tender smile. Even if her marriage to Neil had been a terrible mistake, a decision taken at a time when she had been almost silly with unhappiness, it had still given her Jenny. It hadn't been an entire disaster.

She shut the door of the bedroom carefully behind her and made her way downstairs. The door of the dining room stood open, but Fiona, hovering uncertainly, saw that the only person in the room was a tall, dark-haired girl who was pouring herself a glass of sherry at the sideboard. She paused when she saw Fiona.

'Hello, Fiona! Long time no see!' Then laughing at Fiona's surprised expression, 'Don't you remember me?'

Fiona knit her brows. Margaret Campbell had not prepared her for any other guests in the house. If this pretty dark-haired girl *was* a guest? She seemed very much at home—seemed, too, to expect Fiona to know who she was. But. . . .

The girl flicked back her dark hair and the gesture triggered something in Fiona's memory. 'Good heavens!' she said blankly. '*Judi!*'

Judi grinned. 'That's right. Neil's little cousin. How old was I when you last saw me? Eleven?'

13

'About that. You had long legs and plaits and freckles!' Fiona looked at her, then laughed. 'You've still got the long legs!'

Judi's hazel eyes danced. 'One of my most important assets! How are you, Fiona? It's nice to see you again.'

'Thank you.' If ever there was a case of an ugly duckling being transformed into a swan, Fiona thought, this was it. What had the plain, rather gawky schoolgirl she vaguely remembered got to do with this very attractive, self-possessed young woman?

Judi was surveying her with undisguised interest. 'You're prettier than ever, otherwise I don't think you've changed a scrap. Wait until Bruce sees you! I believe he's got a penchant for honey blondes!'

Fiona stared. 'Bruce?'

'Uncle's factor. He lives in a cottage on the estate.' She paused, then added lightly, 'You really *are* out of touch, aren't you?'

'Yes. Yes, I am. I didn't even know that you were staying here. Nobody ever mentioned it.'

'Oh, it's purely a temporary arrangement! I had a bad bout of 'flu a few weeks ago and the quack said I needed a rest and a change of air. I thought of Aunt Margaret and hey presto! here I am in bonnie Scotland!'

Of course, Fiona thought, Judi's parents lived in London. It was only occasionally, in the old days, that Judi had visited her Scottish relatives. She had been so much younger than Rowan and Neil and Fiona that they'd been apt to regard her as rather a nuisance and to exclude her, as much as possible, from their activities. 'Who wants a kid like that tagging along behind us?' Neil and Rowan had been wont to say crossly, and had made it clear to the indignant Judi

14

that her presence was unwelcome.

Memories swooped and tore. Fiona drew a long breath and said, 'No job to worry about?'

'I'm an actress.' Judi paused, then added with a sort of rueful honesty, 'Not a very successful one. It's ages since I did any work. Luckily my godmother left me quite a bit of money when she died, so I'm not exactly destitute. Bruce thinks it's frightful, living on inherited money, but then he's a bit like that, very dour and moral! *You* don't think it's frightful, do you? After all—' She stopped abruptly and her face went pink.

Fiona raised her brows. 'After all what?'

Judi hesitated. Then she said almost defiantly, 'Well, you and Neil had a daughter, didn't you? She's almost bound to inherit this place one day, there just isn't anyone else except me and I don't really count— not in *that* way, I mean.'

'No?' Fiona asked rather drily. She disliked the turn the conversation had taken, though it was obvious that Judi meant no harm. She looked at the girl again, rather more intently. She was very like Neil, she thought with sudden surprise. The same sparkling brown eyes and wavy dark hair and the same ready smile. For that reason, if for no other, she was probably a favourite with her aunt and uncle, though Margaret had never mentioned her in any of her letters. Not that that was very surprising. Letter-writing didn't come easily either to her or to her husband and their brief communications had always been singularly dull and colourless, completely lacking in local news. And Fiona, for reasons of her own, had never asked questions about anyone.

'Ah, Fiona. You and Judi have renewed your acquaintance, I see.' Margaret Campbell came into the room, followed by her husband, walking slowly and leaning heavily on his stick. 'We thought you'd be glad to find Judi here, Fiona. She'll be company for you, especially as I'm afraid you won't find many of your old friends left.'

Before Fiona could answer Douglas Campbell laid his hand on his niece's shoulder and gave it an affectionate shake.

'If Fiona can manage to keep up with you! Where did you go haring off to this afternoon, lassie? You were driving that Mini of yours as though it was a racing car!'

Judi laughed and wrinkled her nose. 'I went to see, Rowan, of course. It was supposed to be his free afternoon, only unfortunately it didn't work out that way!' She turned to Fiona, who had become very pale. 'At least you've got one old friend left, Fiona—Rowan Macrae. Handsomer than ever and ten times more devastating!'

The silence stretched. Judi, staring, said, 'You *do* remember Rowan, don't you? You can't possibly have forgotten—'

'Of course I remember him.' Fiona was surprised how calm and matter-of-fact her voice sounded. 'I didn't expect him still to be here, though. He—he was training to be a doctor when I knew him. He wanted to specialise in surgery—'

'He's joined his father in the practice instead.' It was Mrs Campbell, not Judi, who answered. 'I know that at one time it wasn't what he really wanted—in fact, I think he turned down a very good job in an Edinburgh hospital—but old Dr Macrae needed help badly. He had a stroke and still has to take great care. He couldn't get a really satisfactory locum, so Rowan stepped into the breach and—well, he's been here ever since.'

' Much to everyone's satisfaction,' Douglas Campbell put in. ' He's got a good head on his shoulders. We're very lucky to have him.'

Judi pouted. ' *I* think he's wasted! He's brilliant, he ought to be doing something really spectacular instead of delivering babies and prescribing pink pills! However, time will tell! His father's a lot better, I'm sure it won't be long before he's able to return to work.'

' Well, we shall see.—Fiona dear, you must be starving!' Margaret Campbell smiled at her daughter-in-law. ' Jenny quite all right?'

' Fast asleep. She must have been terribly tired.' Fiona grasped thankfully at the change of conversation. ' Our rooms are so pretty. Thank you for giving us two adjoining ones.'

' I thought Jenny might like to feel that you were near her. You used not to like being alone in the dark, Fiona, remember?'

' It was about the only thing that did frighten her,' old Mr Campbell said with a laugh. ' What an intrepid trio you were—you and Rowan and Neil! Always up to some kind of mischief!'

The words were followed by a sigh. Fiona saw her mother-in-law glance at a full-length portrait of Neil, hanging on one of the panelled walls, and a little silence fell. It was Judi who broke it. She began plying Fiona with questions and after dinner insisted on accompanying her to her room to talk to her while she was unpacking.

' Gregarious, that's me,' she said cheerfully, perching herself on the foot of Fiona's bed. ' If I talk too much and get on your nerves you can tell me to shut up, though. I promise I won't take offence. I *do* talk too

17

much, I know I do, but luckily some people seem to like it.'

Fiona laughed. 'I'm sure your uncle and aunt enjoy your company.'

'Mmmm. They're dears, aren't they? Isn't it ghastly about Uncle losing his sight? Rowan says that there's only a slight chance that anything can be done for him.'

'It's dreadful. He's always been so active.' Fiona shook out the creases from a blue dress and hung it up in the huge mahogany wardrobe. She hoped that Judi would not realise that it still gave her a queer jolt to hear Rowan referred to so casually. The last thing in the world she'd expected was to find that he was still at Inveray. He'd been so single-minded about his career, so ambitious. . . .

When she turned round she found Judi regarding her thoughtfully. 'I know it's absolutely none of my business, Fiona, but why have you never come home before this? Are you so very happy in America, even —even without Neil?'

Fiona's hesitation was almost imperceptible. 'I have Jenny. Friends. Quite a nice house. Enough money to live on. And a job I like doing.'

'What sort of a job?'

'I do illustrations for children's books. Work that luckily I can do at home.'

'Oh! I'd forgotten that you were artistic.' Judi leaned back, clasping her hands behind her head as she watched Fiona bundle a pile of thick, brightly-coloured sweaters into a drawer. 'Have you never thought of marrying again? Neil's been dead for years and you're only—how old? Twenty-eight? And you're frightfully attractive.'

Fiona coloured vividly. She had thought of marry-

18

ing again—yes. In fact, before her mother-in-law's letter had arrived she'd almost made up her mind to become engaged to a man who had been a close friend for several years. Steve Connaught, the publisher for whom she worked.

Judi saw her change colour and gave a rueful little laugh. 'Have I embarrassed you? Sorry! I guess I oughtn't to ask so many personal questions! Only—well, I may as well be honest. You've always rather intrigued me, Fiona.'

Fiona raised her brows. 'Intrigued you? In what way do you mean?'

'Well, I could never understand why on earth you suddenly decided to marry Neil. I was only a kid at the time, but I'd have betted a year's pocket-money that you weren't particularly keen on him—at least, not in *that* way. I—I suppose you must have been, though. You were just pretty good at hiding your real feelings.'

There was a moment's silence. Then Judi added rather nervously, 'I think just about everyone was shaken absolutely rigid when you and Neil suddenly announced your engagement. It was all so quick! I mean, you were married less than a month afterwards and your honeymoon was the trip to the States! I'm sure there are people in Inveray who still can't quite believe that you really are Mrs Neil Campbell and not Fiona MacAllister from the Manse!'

'They'll believe it all right when they see Jenny.' Fiona spoke more sharply than she had intended. Judi's frankness was a little disconcerting, to say the least of it.

Judi laughed. 'I peeped at her just now, while you were in the bathroom. She looks very sweet. Uncle and Aunt adore her already.'

'She's their only grandchild. They badly wanted

to see her.'

' Then that's why you've come home? Rowan said he thought it might be that.'

Fiona bent over her case. ' You quote Rowan rather a lot. You and he must be pretty good friends. I gather he isn't—married?'

' Heavens, no! He's still a very eligible bachelor. A state of affairs I mean to rectify at the first possible opportunity,' Judi said cheerfully. Then, as Fiona straightened and stared at her, ' At least I'm honest about it! I'm crazy about Rowan, always have been, ever since I was a kid. Only trouble was that until quite recently that's just how he always regarded me. Frustrating, to say the least of it!'

Fiona caught her breath. ' I . . . see.'

' He's coming to dinner tomorrow. Not that I shall see a lot of him, I expect he'll play chess with Uncle. Do you play? They tried to teach me, but even the rudiments of the game were quite beyond me!' Judi leaned down to pick up a skirt that Fiona had dropped. ' I suppose you knew Rowan as well as any-one did. I wonder if you'll find him much changed?'

' Eight years is a long time.'

' I suppose so.' Judi considered. ' I don't think he's quite the same devil-may-care character he used to be: he's tougher, a bit more cynical, but he can still charm a bird off a tree if he feels like it. It's high time he did settle down with a wife and family, though I hope to goodness he won't want to stay in Inveray! It's all right for holidays, but as a permanent thing—!'

' That's how Neil used to talk. You're rather like him, Judi.'

' I suppose I can take that as a compliment? I wasn't very keen on him, you know, even though he was my cousin. It was always Rowan I liked best.

Still, you knew them both a lot better than I did and since it was Neil that you preferred—'

Fiona closed the lid of her case. ' I'm not going to do any more unpacking tonight, Judi. Would you mind terribly if I went to bed? I'm—I'm rather tired and a bit headachey.'

' Oh, gosh, I'm sorry! ' Judi was all compunction. ' I *told* you to shut me up if I talked too much! Do you want an aspirin? I've got some in my room.'

Somehow Fiona managed to smile. ' It's all right, thanks. I've got some of my own. Will you tell your uncle and aunt that I won't be coming down again tonight, Judi? I'm sure they'll understand.'

' Of course they will. Sleep well! I shall look forward to meeting your daughter at breakfast tomorrow morning!'

Judi departed. Without her gay and volatile presence the room seemed strangely quiet and empty. Fiona crossed to the window and sat down upon the broad sill, leaning her aching head against the cold glass. In the distance, the lights of the village glimmered like fairy lanterns among the pines. She stared at them, wondering which one was Rowan Macrae's.

Her hands, gripped tightly together, showed a little of the tension she was feeling. It was absurd . . . ridiculous . . . that Judi's artless revelations should have had such a disturbing effect upon her. Rowan and Judi. What could be more natural or suitable? After all, as she had said to Judi, eight years was a long time. Rowan's wild oats had doubtless all been sown by now. And it was she, Fiona, who had reaped their bitter harvest! She, and a girl named Tessa Mac-Gregor. Tessa, red-haired and sullenly beautiful. . . .

In the bedroom adjoining Jenny turned over. Fiona went quickly to her side and, stooping, straightened

21

the child's body and carefully tucked the blankets around her shoulders. Somehow, in so doing she managed to shake off the tumultuous feelings that had threatened to engulf her. Rowan, like Neil, belonged to the past. It was Jenny, her daughter, who was the future.

CHAPTER II

Fiona woke to brilliant sunshine and the sound of Jenny's small insistent voice. 'Mommy! Mommy, it's time to get up!'

Fiona surfaced reluctantly. For a moment she thought she was in her bedroom in Miami and then her eyes took in her unfamiliar surroundings and realisation dawned. Jenny was standing by the side of her bed, looking down at her. She had dressed herself in a pair of jeans and a scarlet sweater and she was holding her brush and comb in her hand.

Fiona sat up. She glanced at her little bedside clock and gave an exclamation of surprise. 'Goodness, it's nearly eight o'clock!'

Jenny climbed on to the bed and sat with her arms wrapped around her knees. 'I can hear people moving about downstairs and when I opened my door I could smell bacon frying. I guess that means it'll soon be breakfast-time. I'm starving!'

Fiona laughed. 'I expect you are. I'll hurry up and get dressed.'

'Can I go downstairs and start exploring? It looks just marvellous outside!'

'I thought you said you were starving?'

'Just till breakfast's ready, I mean.'

Fiona shook her head. 'I think you'd better wait for me as it's our first morning.' She jumped out of bed and went to the window, throwing it open and leaning out. In her yellow pyjamas, her hair caught back in a pony-tail, she looked very little older than her daughter.

'Nothing's changed.' She spoke softly to herself,

23

shaken once more by memories. The air was crisp, but the sun was warm. She heard the sound of wind moving in the pines, like a distant sea, and saw, through the trees, a gleam of white, where the sunlight struck the sparkling waters of the nearby loch. No wonder Jenny couldn't wait to explore!

Jenny's bright head was at her elbow. 'Isn't it gorgeous, Mommy?'

Fiona laughed and hugged her. 'Indeed it is! And I know just what you mean about being hungry, poppet. So am I!'

'It's the air,' Jenny said wisely. Her voice was full of happiness and Fiona felt an answering singing within herself. She forgot how difficult she'd found it to go to sleep the previous night, despite her tiredness. She forgot how she'd had to fight against the resurrection of old hurts, old resentments. She felt at one with the world. She even sang to herself as she showered and dressed, unaware, just at first, that they had been joined by Judi.

'So you *are* up, Fiona! I wondered.' She looked at Jenny and smiled, her dark eyes crinkling at the corners. 'How d'you do, Miss Campbell? I saw you last night, but you were fast asleep. I'm Judi Conway and I'm staying here, too.'

'Oh!' Jenny returned her gaze. 'Are you *Aunt* Judi?'

'I don't think so. No, of course I'm not! You and I are second cousins,' Judi said cheerfully. And then, 'I've come to tell you breakfast is ready. Are you hungry?'

Fiona, wearing a grey skirt and chunky blue sweater, the sun catching the bright threads of her hair, moved towards them. 'We're both ravenous, aren't we, Jenny? This air—it's pure intoxication!'

Judi laughed. In her black trews and bright scarlet jersey her *gamin* look was cleverly accentuated. 'I have to admit it's an improvement on London! Are you ready, Fiona? Then come and say good morning to your grandparents, Jenny!'

There was porridge for breakfast, as Fiona had guessed there would be, and bacon and eggs and toast and honey. There was even coffee, although Margaret and Douglas Campbell always drank tea. Jenny sat between them and managed, besides eating a huge breakfast, to ask innumerable questions. At one stage Fiona felt obliged to intervene, but Douglas Campbell shook his head smilingly.

'Don't worry, my dear. I'm only too glad that the bairn's interested.'

'I am. I'm going to like it here. I'm going to like it *lots*!' Jenny said happily, and Fiona saw the Campbells exchange satisfied glances.

After breakfast Jenny insisted on an immediate voyage of exploration. Fiona had rather hoped that she would be able to show her daughter her old haunts without an intrusive third, but Judi seemed to take it for granted that they would want her to accompany them. After an initial prick of dismay Fiona managed not to mind. It was almost impossible not to like Judi for her irrepressible *joie de vivre* and she and Jenny were already firm friends.

The latter was full of enthusiasm for her new surroundings. 'Oh, this *is* a pretty place! Aren't the colours bright, Mommy? And what's the smell in the air?'

'A mixture of pine-trees and heather, I think,' Fiona told her. 'Oh, look at those berries!' and she pointed to a couple of mountain ash trees on which clusters of brilliant berries stood out like tongues of flame against their green background.

They were walking along a narrow road which wound down the glen in great loops, with sharp twists and sudden corners. Lined by firs and larch and slender mountain ash, it also had high banks hung with long green ferns and coloured by cushions of brilliant berries stood out like spirals of flame against vast sweep of green, with occasional patches of yellow bracken, and in front of them was the loch. Clear and sparkling, it stretched away to the brown and golden hills of the opposite shore and up to the great blue mountains of the north.

Almost inevitably Fiona found herself thinking of Neil and Rowan. They were part of the landscape, part of her life. All her memories were bound up with those two. Neil, the man she had married, and Rowan, the man whose perfidy had caused her world to collapse around her ears. . . .

'Hurry up, Mommy!' Jenny was dancing along like a golden sprite, impatient to reach the loch. Fiona suddenly found herself saying 'I'll race you!' and Jenny gave a shout of delight and darted away like an arrow. Judi and Fiona were close behind her when she suddenly stopped dead.

'Listen!'

'Listen to what?' Laughing and breathless, Fiona leant against the trunk of a tree and Judi subsided in a heap at her feet as a battered shooting brake poked itself round a bend in the road.

A man was at the wheel and Judi, looking up, gave a quick exclamation. 'Bruce!' She waved and the vehicle drew up alongside.

'Uncle's factor. I told you about him last night,' Judi said, scrambling to her feet as the driver opened the door of the shooting brake, got out and approached them with a slightly diffident air.

Fiona discovered later that Bruce Buchanan was twenty-eight, but he looked rather older He was not particularly handsome, but he had a four-square look to him and a pleasant face redeemed from ordinariness by a pair of keen grey eyes and a remarkably firm chin. He looked strong, dependable and completely unflappable.

Judi performed the necessary introductions rather perfunctorily and Fiona had the feeling that she now regretted her impulsive wave. A hint of coolness had crept into her manner and it was obvious that she did not much care for Bruce even though he, for his part, treated her with amiable politeness.

'I've heard a lot about you from your father-in-law, Mrs Campbell,' he said, taking Fiona's hand in a firm grip. 'He's been looking forward to your visit for weeks. It's practically made a new man of him.'

'Oh, for heaven's sake don't call her Mrs Campbell!' Judi exclaimed. 'I'm sure she'd much rather be Fiona!'

'Yes, I would,' Fiona confessed, smiling. She liked the look of Bruce Buchanan and wondered a little at Judi's rather offhand way of treating him. Of course he wasn't her type, he was much too quiet and reserved, but surely that didn't explain her none too carefully disguised antagonism?

Jenny had been eyeing Bruce thoughtfully. 'What is a factor? What do you do? I don't think we have them in the States, do we, Mommy?' she asked interestedly.

Bruce laughed and began to explain, but Judi interrupted him before he had finished.

'Don't forget to tell her how hard you work, Bruce! Twelve hours a day, seven days a week! You, at least, can never be accused of being a lily of the field!' she said with dangerous sweetness.

There was a gleam in her dark eyes which told Fiona that for some reason she was being deliberately provocative, but though Bruce's lips tightened he answered her calmly.

'Don't make hard work sound such a boring virtue, Judi. Some of us actually enjoy it, you know.'

'Oh well! There's no accounting for tastes, is there?' Judi said, and laughed.

There was an awkward little silence which Fiona hastily rushed to fill.

'You can't think what a relief it is to walk down this road and find that nothing's changed. A friend of mine who's been away from England for the last six or seven years went home recently and found that huge chunks of her home county—Buckinghamshire—had changed out of all recognition. Motorways and concrete jungles where there used to be fields and woods. This '—and she waved her hand at the quiet loch with the mountains towering opposite—' looks just the same as it did before I went away.'

'I'm glad you haven't been disappointed,' Bruce said quietly.

Judi glanced somewhat ostentatiously at her watch. 'Don't let us keep you, Bruce. I suppose you're in your usual mad hurry to do something useful!'

He gave her a brief hard look. 'That isn't quite the way I'd put it myself, but yes, I'd better get moving. I'm sorry that since we're going in opposite directions I can't offer anyone a lift.' He turned to Fiona and smiled. 'I shall look forward to seeing you again. And Jenny too, of course.'

'He's a nice man,' said Jenny as the shooting brake spluttered into life and roared off down the road. 'I like him.'

'Then you haven't yet learnt the art of discrimination,' Judi said tartly, kicking at a stone.

Jenny looked puzzled. 'Dis—? What's that?'

Judi's eyes met Fiona's and she laughed a little ruefully. 'Sorry! I should have known better!' She ruffled Jenny's hair. 'Forget it, chicken. I was just being silly.'

Jenny was too anxious to reach the loch to worry overmuch about grown-ups' obscure remarks. She skipped ahead and was well out of earshot when Fiona turned to Judi and said quietly, 'I gather you're not very keen on Bruce?'

'He's a pompous prig.'

'Oh?' Fiona raised her brows.

Judi glowered. 'All right, I admit I'm prejudiced. It's just that I'm not over-fond of people who say what they think, whether it's pleasant or unpleasant. To be quite honest, I've had a few home truths from Bruce Buchanan and the result is that I'm hopping mad with him!'

Fiona glanced at her, faintly amused. 'Home truths?'

'Bruce thinks I'm idle and frivolous and hopelessly self-centred. I am, of course, but I don't see why I should change. Especially not to suit someone like Bruce, who fairly reeks of hell-fire and righteousness and moral sanctity!' She laughed suddenly. 'I believe that's one of the things I like so much about Rowan. He's quite unshockable. Not surprising, really. You've only got to look at him to realise that he's probably been a bit of a devil himself in his time!'

Fiona thrust her hands into the pockets of her sheepskin jacket. 'I wouldn't know about that.'

'No, I don't suppose you would,' Judi agreed.

' Yours was a purely platonic friendship, wasn't it?'

' Of course.' Fiona kept her voice light and cool. For Rowan's sake, for the sake of her own pride, she had no intention of telling Judi the real truth. Not, in point of fact, that there was so very much to tell. Theirs *had* been a platonic friendship until that day on the mountains . . . the day she'd fallen and Rowan, shaken for once out of his usual calm, had picked her up and cradled her in his arms and told her that he loved her. Holding her close, he'd kissed her in a way that had turned her bones to water, and she'd known then what before she had always refused to acknowledge . . . that she loved Rowan, had loved him since she was nine years old and he'd risked a wetting to pull her out of the loch. For perhaps a week she had tasted absolute happiness. Then . . . disillusionment. Disillusionment that even now she could hardly bear to think about. . . .

Judi glanced at her curiously. ' It might have been different, I suppose, if there hadn't been Neil. When exactly did you find out that you were in love with him, Fiona? When he said he was going to America and you realised that you might not see him again for years and years?'

Somehow Fiona managed a shaky laugh. ' Judi! It all happened so long ago——'

' Which, being rightly interpreted, means that you don't want to talk about it,' Judi said with a flash of shrewdness. ' All right, Fiona, I won't tease. I do realise that you must have loved Neil an awful lot or you'd hardly have remained faithful to his memory all these years, would you?'

Fiona was spared the necessity of replying because just at that moment Jenny stumbled and fell, grazing her knee. She didn't cry, but Fiona put her arm round her and kept up a comforting flow of chatter as they approached a small cluster of houses by the lochside.

Built of grey stone and with gardens full of autumn flowers, the houses were set along the road which ran by the side of the loch. Above were masses of dark trees and above these the open greenhill, with an occasional shoulder of grey rock or great purple patch of heather.

'There's the post office, Jenny, and next to it is the kirk. That funny little building over there is the village school. Or it used to be.' Fiona, resolutely pushing all thoughts of Rowan to the back of her mind, spoke eagerly.

'Oh, and there's a boat, with someone in it!' Jenny was dancing up and down with excitement. 'Can we go on the loch, Mommy? In a little boat just like that?'

'Another day, perhaps,' Fiona told her.

'You must ask Rowan for the loan of his launch,' Judi said casually. 'I'm sure he wouldn't mind.'

Fiona stiffened. 'I wouldn't dream—'

Judi was looking in another direction and did not let her finish. 'In fact, you can ask him now. There's his car, outside that house there. And—yes, there's Rowan, talking to old Mrs MacGillivray. I believe her husband's got a broken ankle. I was with Rowan yesterday when the call came through.'

Fiona felt rather as though someone had kicked her in the solar plexus. She'd known ever since the previous evening that she'd have to meet Rowan some time. Only she'd banked on having time to prepare herself, to school her face into a mask of polite indifference. And she hadn't—oh, she hadn't!—wanted to meet him here, by the side of the loch!

Her heart hammering against her ribs, she turned

31

slowly and reluctantly followed Judi's gaze. As she did so a tall, broad-shouldered man in shabby tweeds strode towards them from the open doorway of one of the grey houses. He walked with an easy, loose-limbed grace, his dark hair glistening with an almost reddish cast in the bright sun. Fiona thought, 'He hasn't changed . . . not really,' and her mouth went dry.

'Hello, Judi.' Rowan smiled at the girl who went eagerly forward to greet him. Then his eyes found Fiona's. 'Welcome home, Fiona.'

'I needn't have worried,' Fiona thought. There was nothing in Rowan's dark blue eyes, nothing in his voice, except polite, almost detached friendliness. And after all, why should there be anything else? As she herself had said, eight years was a long time. . . .

She drew a deep breath. 'Thank you, Rowan. It's nice to be back.'

Safe, banal phrases. Judi, animated, sparkling, put her hand on Rowan's arm.

'Jenny wants to go out on the loch, Rowan. I've told her and Fiona that I'm sure you'll lend them your launch.'

'Jenny?' Rowan raised his brows and then smiled as Jenny came forward and stood regarding him gravely. 'Of course. I'd know her anywhere as your daughter, Fiona.'

'You're the man who pulled my mommy out of the loch.' Jenny knew one thing, and one thing only, about the tall man smiling down at her and she had no hesitation in repeating it.

'Jenny!' Fiona exclaimed, flushing hotly as Rowan tilted an amused eyebrow in her direction.

'Did I, Jenny? Then that's one good deed to my credit, anyway,' he said lazily.

'Only one, my handsome hero?' Judi chaffed.

Rowan's lean brown face wore a somewhat cynical expression. 'Hardly a hero, I think, Judi. If I did pull Fiona out of the loch—and I really can't remember the incident!—I feel reasonably sure that the minimum amount of danger and discomfort was involved!'

Jenny was regarding Rowan with astonishment. 'Why can't you remember? Have you got a bad memory for things like that?'

'I think I must have,' Rowan said with mock gravity. 'But I promise I won't forget that you'd like to go on the loch. I think that could quite easily be arranged, Jenny.'

'Oh, *thank* you!' Jenny's voice was ecstatic and Judi laughed.

'You've made a conquest, Rowan.' She turned to Fiona. 'Well, do you think he's changed much? Yes or no?'

There was no mistaking the faintly proprietorial note in her voice. 'This man is mine,' it seemed to say.

'Not really.' It was quite easy, Fiona discovered with surprise, to match Rowan's nonchalance, though her tension remained. She added, smiling, 'Perhaps you've put on a bit of weight, Rowan, but it suits you.'

He regarded her coolly, almost enigmatically. 'And you look charming,' he said. 'More beautiful than ever.'

The compliment came easily, but Fiona seemed to see a certain mockery on his lips. He *had* changed—far more than at first she'd thought. Rowan the boy had always been a creature of quick moods, the weather of his spirit changeable and unpredictable, but this smiling cynicism was something altogether different. And oddly disturbing. She could well

W L—B

believe that coupled with his lean vitality it made him almost irresistibly attractive to many women.

Judi put her hand up to her hair to push back a straying tendril. 'How's your patient this morning, Rowan?'

'Fairly comfortable, thank you. He's lucky, it was a clean break.' He paused. 'Mrs MacGillivray recognised you at once, Fiona, eight years or no eight years. She knows it's your first morning at Inveray, but she wondered if you'd have time to stop by and have a word with her.'

'Of course!' Fiona spoke warmly. She'd meant to do that, anyway, for Mrs MacGillivray was someone else who was part of her childhood. A stalwart of the kirk, she'd been sorry for the minister's motherless daughter and had gone out of her way to be kind to her. Many of the delicious scones and cakes for which she'd been justly famous had made their way to the Manse ... and many a bag of homemade toffee or fudge had been pressed into Fiona's small, sunburnt hands when she'd come to play by the loch.

Judi hesitated. 'You don't particularly want me to come with you, do you, Fiona? I saw Mrs MacGillivray yesterday and if Rowan's going up the Glen I rather thought I might beg a lift.'

'Any time,' Rowan said, smiling at her.

In spite of herself Fiona's mind flew back to the many times that Rowan had put the child Judi in her place, told her to run away and get lost and not to be a nuisance. Only that had been the child Judi, not this vivid young woman with her laughing dark eyes and bewitching smile!

She said quickly, 'That's all right, Judi. We'll see you at lunchtime, I expect.'

The four of them walked over to the MacGillivrays'

house. Rowan and Judi got into the car and the former raised his hand in a brief, unsmiling salute before driving off down the loch road. Jenny stood looking after them until Fiona addressed her rather sharply.

'Stop dreaming, Jenny! We're going to say hello to someone who used to be very kind to me when I was a little girl of your age.'

Mrs MacGillivray, hospitable to the core, more than made up for Rowan's somewhat unenthusiastic welcome. She enveloped first Fiona, and then Jenny, in a warm hug and ushered them into a small but spotless living room where a cheerful fire glowed in the grate and bright rugs of hooked rag covered the floor. Her husband, his injured ankle propped up on a footstool, was sitting in a rocking chair. A shy, reserved man of few words, he was content to smile a greeting, though he managed a few gruff words when Fiona expressed sympathy with his injury.

Mrs MacGillivray, plump and rosy-cheeked, with soft, silvery hair, placed a huge plate of scones on the table and bustled around making coffee in a huge earthenware jug.

'Eh, Miss Fiona, ye're as bonny as ever!' she said with honest satisfaction. 'And your little lass is jest like you!' She smiled at Jenny. ''Tis high time ye coom hame, ma wean!'

If Jenny didn't altogether understand the words she understood the tone of voice. 'I like Scotland!' she said with conviction.

Mrs MacGillivray chuckled. ''Tis gled I am to hear it!' She looked reproachfully at Fiona. 'Ye should ha' coom hame when Maister Neil died, Miss Fiona. I didna' think ye'd iver prefair America to Scotland!'

Fiona's throat was tight. 'I didn't, not really, Mrs MacGillivray. It was just . . . somehow it seemed easier

35

to stay put.'

Mrs MacGillivray sighed. 'Nae doot! Nae doot! Puir lassie! How I felt for ye when the news coom to us! The Laird ... puir man, he's niver been the same since! How d'ye find him, Miss Fiona?'

'He seems to be in quite good spirits, all things considered.'

'I'm told he'll gae blind in a few months' time. If even the young doctor canna do naethin' to help him. ...' Mrs MacGillivray did not finish her sentence but sighed and shook her head sadly.

Fiona stared down at the steaming cup of coffee that had been placed before her. 'It seems funny to hear you refer to "the young doctor". Everyone used to think the world of old Dr Macrae!'

'And 'tis the world we think o' the young doctor too, ye ken!' Mrs MacGillivray said briskly. 'We hoped mebbe he'd stay, but. ...' She shook her head again.

No, Fiona thought, it wasn't likely that Rowan would stay. Especially if he married Judi. She would never be happy for long in Inveray.

It was well over an hour before she and Jenny were able to tear themselves away from Mrs MacGillivray's hospitable clutches, and by the time they arrived back at Cragside lunch was almost ready.

'Well, have you heard all the village gossip?' Mrs Campbell asked with a grim little smile. 'There's not much that goes on hereabouts that Maggie MacGillivray doesn't get to hear about, sooner or later!'

Fiona laughed. 'I heard quite a lot, yes, but most of the names she mentioned were quite new to me. I suppose they were just small children when I left Inveray.' She hesitated, then added with would-be casualness, 'There's somebody I meant to ask about,

36

only I forgot. What's happened to Tessa MacGregor? Is she still living in Inveray?'

'No. She's got a good job in Glasgow, I haven't seen her for years.' Mrs Campbell hesitated, then added half unwillingly, 'She hasn't had an easy time, poor lassie. She had a bairn, you know, six or seven months after you and Neil went off to America, and her father was so upset and angry he disowned her. Did you never hear about it?'

Fiona was standing very still. After a moment she shook her head, and her mother-in-law sighed.

'You can imagine the furore there was! Dear knows who the baby's father was, Tessa would never tell, though Duncan MacGregor did his level best to make her. She's stubborn, that girl: she always was, even as a child.'

Fiona drew a long breath. 'Is she—did she keep the baby?'

'It died soon after it was born, poor wee thing. I believe Tessa was very ill for quite a long time afterwards, too. It was Dr Macrae who was her Good Samaritan. I believe he arranged for her to stay with some nice people and helped her financially too, I shouldn't wonder. I know for a fact he gave Duncan MacGregor a piece of his mind for turning his back on the girl, but it made no difference. Perhaps if Jessie MacGregor had lived . . . but she died, five or six years back.'

'Wasn't—isn't there a little boy?'

'Aye, Robbie. He's nearly ten now, lives alone with his father. I doubt if Tessa would come back now even if she were asked. From all accounts she's done well for herself, though she doesn't seem to be interested in getting married. Disillusioned, probably. She was a nice enough girl despite all her wild ways and I have no doubt she was more sinned against than sinning.'

The knife she was using slipped from Fiona's grasp and clattered against the sink. Her mother-in-law, glancing towards her, spoke sharply.

'You've cut yourself, child: just look at your finger . . . hold it under the cold tap, that'll stop the bleeding. I'll finish slicing those tomatoes.'

'The knife slipped,' Fiona said a little breathlessly. It was her own fault. She hadn't been concentrating.

'Where's Jenny?' Mrs Campbell raised her voice to make herself heard over the noise of the running tap.

Fiona looked out of the window. 'With Judi in the garden. They're playing some sort of hide and seek from the look of things.'

Mrs Campbell frowned. 'I don't quite know what to make of Judi. She's nearly twenty-one, but she seems to me to be so immature.'

'She's very attractive.'

'Oh, she's *that* all right. And a bit of a baggage into the bargain! Has she told you that she means to marry Rowan Macrae?'

'Yes. She did tell me that.'

Mrs Campbell pursed her lips. 'This modern generation! I don't give much for her chances. Rowan seems attracted to her, but—'

'But what?'

'But he's a good-looking young man and if he's not married it's not because he's not already had plenty of chances!' Mrs Campbell said drily. 'Frankly, I don't think myself that Rowan is at all anxious to take on the responsibility of a wife and family. From all accounts he's had any number of girl-friends these last few years, but he's never shown the slightest sign of

38

wanting to settle down with any one of them. He likes Judi, I'm sure, and they've been seeing quite a lot of each other, but—'

Fiona carefully dried her finger, which had stopped bleeding. 'I don't think you need worry too much. I thought when I saw them together this morning that Rowan seemed very fond of her.'

'I hope you're right. I wouldn't like him to break her heart.'

Fiona nearly said, 'Breaking hearts is a speciality of Rowan's. Didn't you know?' but she didn't. Instead she said in a carefully non-committal voice, 'I don't suppose he will.'

'Will what?' demanded a gay voice, and Judi strolled into the kitchen, followed by a flushed and breathless Jenny.

'Oh, it's nothing important! You've got leaves and twigs all over your sweater, Judi, did you know?'

'I didn't, but I'm not in the least surprised. I crawled under a bush to hide from your infant. She tells me she's enjoyed her morning. I hope you have too, Fiona?'

'Yes, thank you.'

Judi turned to her aunt. 'Oh, I didn't tell you. We saw Bruce this morning, so I made him stop and introduced him to Fiona.'

'You needn't have bothered, dear.' Mrs Campbell's voice was placid. 'She would have seen him tonight anyway. He's coming to dinner, as well as Rowan.'

Judi groaned. 'Oh, lor'! That means that after Uncle and Rowan have played chess someone's bound to suggest a game of bridge! Do you play, Fiona?'

''Fraid not.'

'Neither does Rowan. I can play moderately well, but Bruce is paralysingly good! It's about his only

39

social accomplishment!'

'Mr Buchanan is a very nice young man,' her aunt said repressively, and though Judi pulled a face, she wisely said no more.

CHAPTER III

That evening Fiona read Jenny a story and tucked her up before going into her own room to change from sweater and skirt into a dress for dinner. Rowan, she knew, had already arrived. She'd heard his deep voice in the hall below and Judi's answering, clear and eager.

In no hurry to join them, Fiona had purposely lingered over her goodnights to Jenny and she took more time than usual over her hair and make-up. When she had finished she stared critically at her reflection in the mirror. 'You're more beautiful than ever,' Rowan had said, but had he meant it? If he remembered anything of the girl Fiona he must surely remember that she had had eyes which sparkled and a mouth that had smiled easily. This reflected face had a faintly wistful expression and eyes that were deeply and maternally anxious.

She sighed involuntarily and turned away from the mirror. She couldn't dilly-dally much longer. Perhaps by now Bruce Buchanan would have arrived and she'd be able to talk to him, thus leaving Rowan entirely to Judi!

It didn't work out quite like that. When Fiona came downstairs she opened the drawing-room door on Douglas Campbell discussing with Bruce and Rowan some local problem connected with fishing rights. They all stopped talking the moment she entered the room and she found herself being appraised by three pairs of eyes. Douglas Campbell's were kind, Bruce's shyly admiring and Rowan's . . . Rowan's dark blue gaze revealed nothing.

'Please do go on with your conversation.' She smiled

at her father-in-law as he handed her a glass of sherry. 'I'm quite content to listen.'

'Then you aren't like most of your sex,' Bruce told her with the ghost of a smile.

Fiona laughed. 'I learnt the value of silence at a very early age! I can remember Neil and Rowan threatening to box my ears if I utttered as much as a squeak while they were fishing or bird-watching!'

She spoke with assumed lightness, willing Rowan's face to relax into a smile, but it didn't. He looked, if anything, slightly bored. In a well-cut suit and silk shirt, he looked very different from the way he'd looked earlier in the day. It had been easy on that occasion for Fiona to identify the man with the boy she had known, but she wondered now how she could have been fooled into thinking that the years had dealt with him lightly.

Standing quietly to one side, sipping her sherry and listening to the rise and fall of the three pleasant voices, she had a good opportunity to study his face and to note the suggestion of bitterness about his mouth . . . his curiously shuttered expression and the wariness of his eyes. Then he turned his head and caught her looking at him, and the way his mouth went down at one corner sent the colour flying into her cheeks. Hastily she turned to Bruce and said the first thing that came into her head.

'Where's Judi, do you know?'

'She was called away to the telephone. Mrs Campbell said her father wanted to speak to her.' He paused, then added, 'Maybe he wants to know when she's going back to London.'

Douglas Campbell overheard his remark and laughed. 'You sound rather as if you'd like to know that yourself, Bruce, but we're in no hurry to lose her.

42

She seems to enjoy being here and she makes herself useful in lots of ways. She's taking me to Edinburgh next week, for instance, and though her driving will doubtless result in my sprouting a few more grey hairs, I'm grateful for her help. My wife can't drive, as you know, and of course as things are I mustn't.'

He spoke in a perfectly matter-of-fact way and Fiona paid a silent tribute to his courage. She had already learned from her mother-in-law that he had long ago come to terms with the fact that he was slowly losing his sight. He was the sort of man who would never indulge in self-pity . . . a stoic in every sense of the word.

'Dinner's ready, everyone!' Judi, slim and vibrant in an apricot-coloured woollen dress, appeared in the doorway and the little group passed in procession to the dining room.

Fiona found herself sitting next to Bruce and opposite Rowan and Judi. The table looked beautiful, with its shining silver, lighted candles and flowers, and Margaret had cooked a superb meal. The talk at dinner was good, too, for Douglas Campbell was an excellent conversationalist and could draw others out as skilfully and easily as he could talk himself.

After dinner, as Judi had gloomily predicted, Douglas Campbell suggested a game of bridge. His niece pulled a face behind his back but meekly acquiesced when Bruce asked her to be his partner.

'As Fiona and Rowan aren't bridge players they must entertain each other,' Margaret said, smiling. 'I'm sure they've got a lot to talk about.'

Rowan sat down beside Fiona on the old-fashioned settle. 'Have we?' he asked her mockingly. She met his glance and felt the old, almost-forgotten sensation of swinging away into space.

43

She racked her brains for an answer. Once there had never been any awkward silences between her and Rowan. Even when they hadn't had very much to say to each other they'd always been companionable. Now, what had happened eight years ago had made them strangers. There was nothing left of the links which, forged in childhood, had lasted throughout adolescence. Until Rowan himself had destroyed them. . . .

She felt a sudden urge to say, 'Why did you do it, Rowan? Why did you tell me that I was the only girl you had ever loved when it simply wasn't true? Why did you break my heart into a million little pieces?' but she knew that those questions could never be asked out loud. She would never be able to tell him what she had seen and heard by the loch on that chill October day when mist had blanketed the glen. It had been impossible eight years ago: it was doubly impossible now.

Rowan's brows rose quizzically. 'Penny for your thoughts.'

'They're not for sale.' She accepted the cigarette he handed her, adding flippantly as he took one himself, 'Aren't doctors supposed to set a good example? By not smoking, I mean?'

He looked amused. 'I advise my patients to do as I say, not to do as I do. Besides, I'm not a heavy smoker.'

He held out his lighter and his eyes met hers over the leaping flame. When he next spoke his tone had subtly altered. 'I'm glad you've come home at last, Fiona. I suppose you know that you've made two people very happy?'

'Yes. I realise that.' Fiona looked past him, at her father-in-law's splendid head. Behind him the mellow brown and gold of the books he loved so much

44

glinted in the firelight. On impulse she said, 'Rowan, is there really no more than a slight chance that his sight can be saved?'

Rowan stubbed out the cigarette that he had only just lit. 'I'm afraid not. I'd like to be more optimistic, but the odds are very much against him.'

Fiona bit her lip. 'Miracles happen sometimes.'

'They do, but not often. However, I want your father-in-law to see another specialist next month, a man who has had some brilliant successes in America. If even he says the case is hopeless. . . .' He shrugged and left his sentence unfinished.

Fiona looked down at her hands. 'I feel now that— that I ought to have come home before.'

'Yes. Why didn't you?'

The bluntness of the question took her by surprise. '*Because of you*,' she wanted to say, and wondered what his reaction would be if she did.

'Oh, I don't know . . . it just never seemed to be the right moment. I had to try hard to combine a job with looking after Jenny . . . there always seemed so much to be done. . . .' She paused, then added hastily in case he should think that she was inviting his sympathy, 'I had a good life. I suppose I was selfish, I didn't want anything to disrupt it.'

A pause. Then Rowan said very quietly, 'It must have been a heavy blow, losing Neil so soon after your marriage. I was sorry about that, Fiona, even though I didn't write to you to say so. I should have done.'

'I had lots of sympathetic letters. They—didn't bring him back.'

Rowan shot her a quick look. 'You've changed, Fiona.'

She forced herself to answer lightly. 'Of course. Haven't you?'

45

'Touché.' Rowan suddenly sounded rather bored. He was looking at Judi, whose lovely, vivid face was unusually serious as she studied her cards. How he must wish he wasn't stuck with me!' thought Fiona, and said in a bright, social voice, 'Tell me about yourself. What have you been doing with yourself all these years? I was sure that by now you'd be an eminent surgeon at a famous hospital, with a huge house, a beautiful wife and all the other trappings of success!'

Rowan laughed. 'That sounds like one of those fairy stories you used to be so fond of! You were an authority on witches and gnomes and spells and enchanted castles at one time, remember?'

Fiona refused to be sidetracked. 'I've heard that you turned down a marvellous job in order to come here and help your father.'

Rowan looked momentarily annoyed. 'Then you shouldn't believe all that you hear.'

Fiona was silent. Rowan seemed to have had no difficulty in putting his loyalty to his father before his own personal ambitions. Perhaps he regretted the fact that he had not always been prepared to act with such highmindedness. . . .

When Rowan next spoke there was a faint gleam in his blue eyes which she found oddly disconcerting. 'As for the beautiful wife with whom you endowed me . . . oh no, Fiona! Once bitten, twice shy. I was at a very impressionable age when you jilted me, you know. I've never been able to believe in women since.'

Fiona felt her cheeks burn. This was taking the war into the enemy's camp with a vengeance! 'D-don't be silly!'

He regarded her blandly. 'Do you know, you look positively embarrassed! I'm only joking, my dear. Quite frankly, until a few moments ago I'd done my best to forget that we once exchanged deathless vows on the slopes of Ben Leithen Dui! Only they weren't as deathless as all that, were they? Only a week later, if my memory serves me rightly, you wrote to me to tell me that you were marrying Neil!'

'Rowan—'

His eyes were steady and penetrating. 'I have very bad taste, raking up your past indiscretions like this! Is that what you're going to tell me? Because if so, you're quite right. I am being thoroughly ungentlemanly!'

Fiona clenched her hands in her lap. Her head buzzed with the answers she would have liked to have made, but before she could say anything at all her mother-in-law called to her across the room.

'Fiona dear, would you mind making some more coffee while we finish this rubber?'

'Of course.' Fiona jumped to her feet, thankful that Rowan made no attempt to follow her into the big, old-fashioned kitchen with its red-tiled floor, chintz curtains and well-scrubbed table. She leant against the white porcelain sink, trying desperately to stop herself from trembling. It was all over—all done with! Where was the sense in being angry?

'Let him make a joke of it!' she thought bitterly. 'Be glad he never knew how much he hurt you! Never let him know that the only reason you wrote that letter was because you'd accidentally stumbled on his sordid little secret. . . .'

She picked up the electric kettle and turned on the tap. As the water gushed out her mind flew back willy-nilly to the day that, climbing down the rough path which had led to the side of the loch, she'd come across Rowan and the red-haired girl who was with him. They were talking in loud, angry voices, too absorbed in themselves to realise that they were not alone . . . that Fiona stood staring at them in shocked disbelief.

Tessa's slim, sunburnt hands had been gripping Rowan's arms. Sometimes in her dreams Fiona saw again the girl's beautiful, anguished face, heard her passionate beseeching voice.

'I'm no' asking ye to marry me, Rowan Macrae, only to help me! Ye dinna seem to understand that I canna hae the child! I canna! Do something—oh, do something! Please, Rowan. . . .'

The water spilled over the sides of the kettle. She'd filled it far too full, Fiona thought dully. She turned away from the sink, remembering how that day . . . the day her world had turned to cinders . . . the tears had spilled anyhow down her cheeks all the stumbling way home. Rowan . . . and Tessa MacGregor! Beautiful, wild Tessa with her voluptuous figure and the rebellious streak in her character that had caused her to be in and out of trouble ever since Fiona could remember. . . .

Of course Rowan hadn't wanted to marry her! Beautiful though she was, she was no wife for an ambitious young doctor. Tessa herself hadn't seemed to expect it. But in her desperation she *had* thrown herself on her lover's mercy and it had been painfully obvious to Fiona that Rowan had no intention of doing anything whatsoever to help her. Not that she'd stayed long enough to hear more than his horrified, 'For God's sake, Tessa, you don't know what you're saying! I can't help you . . . you know I can't. . . .'

Later, heartbroken, desolate, unable to think clearly, Fiona had gone alone up into the hills. It was there that Neil found her.

Gently he had asked her the reason for her tears.

48

'Is it Rowan?' Then, as she had not answered, 'Tell me, Fiona. You can trust me, you know that.'

She had never had the confidence in Neil that she had had in Rowan, but he was still her friend. And Rowan's. Surely Neil would know if. . . .

White-faced, despairing, she had asked him point-blank if it was true that Rowan and Tessa had been having an affair. At first he had prevaricated, then unwillingly he had admitted the truth. He'd known about the relationship, he said, for months. . . .

He must have guessed from the expression on her face that her unhappiness was almost too great to bear. Patiently, bit by bit, he had extracted the whole story from her. Then, instead of proffering sympathy, he had almost stunned her by asking her to marry him.

'I've been crazy about you for ages, Fiona, but I never thought I stood a chance,' he'd said, and then he'd added, a little bitterly, 'You always made it clear that you preferred Rowan.'

Bewildered, she had stared at him. 'But . . . Neil! I—I don't love you! I'm fond of you, of course, but—'

'Then that's enough. Marry me, Fiona, and come to America with me. Forget about Rowan and let me take care of you. I want to, so badly. Give me a chance to make you happy. . . .' And then, 'If you aren't here perhaps Rowan will do the decent thing by Tessa and marry her.'

It was that argument that had clinched the matter. She had told Neil that she would marry him and then gone home to write to Rowan, telling him that she'd discovered that she did not really love him and that it had been Neil all the time. She had never received an answer. And he hadn't come to their wedding. That might have caused considerable comment had it not been for the fact that it was such a hurried affair that quite a lot of people had been unable to attend. Even Neil's parents had been bewildered by the speed with which everything was happening and possibly a little worried too.

'It *is* a pity that you're having to get married in such a rush! Why *didn't* you make up your minds sooner?' Mrs Campbell had lamented. 'There isn't time to do anything properly!'

Fiona never knew whether the older woman dimly suspected that she was marrying her son for all the wrong reasons. If she did, she kept her own counsel. She had always been fond of Fiona, and was probably relieved that at least Neil was marrying a Scottish girl and not an American. And of course Neil's own happiness and excitement had been infectious. A little of it had even rubbed off on Fiona, who had made up her mind to put Rowan out of her heart and out of her thoughts forever. Only it hadn't been that easy. . . .

Rowan appeared in the doorway, tall and lazily relaxed. 'You've been a long time. Want any help?'

'No, thanks. At least—you can carry this tray in for me, please.'

He gave her a sharp look as he moved towards her. 'Anything wrong?'

'No. What makes you think there might be?'

His eyes were mocking. 'A certain coolness in your voice. Whatever we were to each other once, you don't like me very much now, do you, Fiona?'

She forced herself to answer calmly. 'I haven't really given the matter much thought. I certainly don't like to be reminded of the . . . mistakes . . . I made in my youth. Who does?'

Rowan threw back his head and laughed. 'In your youth indeed! Don't talk as if you were an old lady, Fiona! You're—how old? Twenty-seven? Twenty-

50

eight? Still a mere child, at any rate!'

'I *have* a child! Remember?' Fiona flared.

His expression suddenly changed. 'Yes.' He paused, then added quietly, 'I don't think anyone who has met Jenny is likely to forget her. She's a delightful little girl. You must be very proud of her.'

This time there was no mockery at all in his voice. Confused, uncertain, she put her hand up to her hair to push back a straying tendril.

Rowan's eyes followed her movement. 'She looks a lot like you. The same colour hair . . . the same eyes. I only met her briefly, but I couldn't see anything of Neil in her at all.'

'She is a little like him, I think.' It was Fiona's turn to pause before adding ruefully, 'Neil badly wanted a son. I'm afraid he might have been very disappointed if—if he'd lived.'

'Nonsense. I expect you'd have given him a son next time round. You always used to say that you wanted at least four children.'

She said involuntarily, 'So did you!' and could then have bitten out her tongue.

The mocking gleam had returned to his eyes. 'Very true. So I did. An inconvenient ambition for a confirmed bachelor. I shall really have to forget my inhibitions regarding holy matrimony and get cracking, won't I?'

Fiona did not reply. Bitterness almost choked her. She was remembering what her mother-in-law had said about Tessa MacGregor. Tessa, whose baby had died shortly after it was born. . . .

She picked up the tray on which she had piled the coffee cups and saucers and almost thrust it into Rowan's hands. Lean brown hands with the long, sensitive fingers of the born surgeon. . . .

51

'Carry that in for me, please. I'll take the coffee.'

Judi looked up as she entered the room. 'We've finished our game. I was just coming to find you! What have you two been doing—enjoying a walk down Memory Lane?' she demanded, laughing.

It was Rowan, following close behind Fiona, who answered.

'"Enjoying" is hardly the right word, Judi. I'm afraid that Fiona finds my memory for—er—past escapades a trifle inconvenient!'

His voice was bland. Fiona could cheerfully have hit him, but luckily her father-in-law chuckled appreciatively.

'That's the worst of two people growing up together! What's he been reminding you of, Fiona— the day you ate so many sour apples off one of my trees that your poor father thought you had appendicitis? Or the night that Neil—the young monkey!—dared you to walk through the churchyard at midnight and you almost caught pneumonia sitting on a tombstone waiting for the church clock to strike the hour?'

If that had been all! thought poor Fiona. Willing herself not to look at Rowan, who was doubtless enjoying her discomfiture, she said hurriedly, 'I don't think it would do for Jenny to hear some of those tales! She's led a comparatively blameless life so far!'

'Och, don't worry about that! There's time, there's time!' said Douglas Campbell, filling his pipe. 'But you weren't a really naughty child, Fiona, far from it. Just a harum-scarum tomboy, eh, Rowan?'

Before Rowan could answer Margaret Campbell said quietly, 'A happy childhood is a wonderful heritage. Don't you agree, Bruce?'

She turned, smiling, to her husband's factor to draw him into the conversation, which to Fiona's great relief

52

became general.

Bruce, despite his shyness, was a man of intelligence and humour, Fiona decided as she listened to him telling an anecdote about a local farmer. He lacked Rowan's striking good looks and Rowan's easy charm, but he was not without a certain amount of distinction. She studied his rugged face, with its slightly crooked nose and determined jaw, with interest and then blushed violently as, turning her head, she realised that Rowan was surveying her sardonically. Their eyes met and he grinned, a derisive little grin which made her seethe inwardly.

'Damn the man!' she thought furiously. 'Hasn't he upset me enough already? Why doesn't he concentrate on Judi? Goodness only knows that's what she wants him to do!'

Judi did, indeed, make her interest in Rowan rather plain. From her point of view, however, it was obviously not a very successful evening, for try as she might she did not succeed in monopolising his attention. He was certainly charming to her, but there was no special warmth in his manner and Fiona could not help feeling sorry for Judi's disappointment.

Although it was illogical, she blamed Rowan. 'He's got a cruel streak,' she thought, writhing inwardly as she recalled the way he had baited her earlier in the evening. 'I suppose he must always have had it.'

And yet was that really true? Rowan, as a boy and then as a young man, had been chary of wearing his heart on his sleeve. His light, almost mocking manner had acted as a kind of defensive barrier, but on occasion an unexpected act of thoughtfulness had made his friends realise that there was a side to his character which he was usually careful to keep hidden. That day on Ben Leithen Dui . . . the day he'd taken her in his arms and told her that he loved her . . . she'd been almost overwhelmed by the depth of his tenderness!

She winced hurriedly away from the intrusive memory. She'd been so young, incapable, no doubt, of making a true judgment. At any rate there'd been no tenderness for poor, desperate Tessa, who'd needed it so badly. . . .

Later in the evening, when Rowan and Bruce had both left and Judi had gone forlornly upstairs to have a bath, Margaret Campbell said quietly, ' All that talk tonight about happy childhoods, Fiona, made me wish more than ever that you would allow little Jenny to grow up here, at Inveray. I know that you have made your home in America, I know you are planning to return in a few weeks' time, but it will be very hard to let you both go.'

She paused, then added wistfully, ' The house is more than big enough for us all. If you stayed you'd have perfect freedom, my dear, to do exactly as you wish. And one day, as you've probably guessed, Cragside will belong to Jenny. If she could learn to love it now. . . .'

Fiona, who had been drinking a cup of hot chocolate, set the mug down carefully and looked at her in-laws in dismay. What could she say to them to make them understand? How could she tell them that she knew, after tonight, that she could never, never make her home in Inveray? Not, at any rate, if Rowan Macrae was staying. . . .

She said slowly, selecting her words with great care, ' It's sweet and kind and dear of you both to want us. I appreciate it, really I do. In some ways it would be absolutely marvellous, but—' The rest of her sentence stuck in her throat. She couldn't bring herself to finish it.

Her father-in-law leant forward and patted her hand. 'Don't fret, lassie. I think I know what's wrong. I was watching your face tonight. Here, you're surrounded by memories of Neil . . . and they hurt. Isn't that so, Fiona?'

Fiona bent her head, the tears pricking her eyelids. Douglas Campbell was right . . . but only partly right. The memories did hurt, but only because she couldn't help regretting that her tragically brief marriage hadn't been happier. Somehow, because of her love for Rowan, who hadn't deserved it, she had completely failed poor Neil. He'd had her loyalty, her affection and her unquestioning support in everything he did, but the one thing he'd wanted above all else she'd been powerless to give him. It was no comfort to tell herself that he'd known right from the first that she did not love him. He'd obviously expected that her feelings would undergo a change after they were married and he'd been bitterly disappointed because they hadn't. . . .

'We won't tease you, Fiona,' Margaret said gently. 'You may change your mind in the next few weeks. If you do, you'll make us very, very happy. And if you don't'—she smiled and sighed at one and the same time—'I can only hope that there will be many other visits. America is a long way away, but at least there are such things as aeroplanes, thank goodness!'

'For a woman who's frightened to death of flying that's quite an admission!' Douglas Campbell said, deliberately lightening the atmosphere.

Margaret and Fiona both laughed and the conversation was changed. A few minutes later Fiona said goodnight and was on her way to her bedroom when she met Judi coming out of the bathroom.

Wearing a pink bath-robe, her soft dark hair curling in damp little tendrils on her face and neck, Judi looked very young and curiously vulnerable. She said, following Fiona into her bedroom, 'Wasn't tonight a drag? I could have screamed at Bruce when he was telling that boring story about that dreadful old farmer, couldn't you?'

'Oh, Judi, be fair!' Fiona protested, laughing. 'It was a very funny story. You couldn't have been listening properly.'

'I wasn't. I was feeling fed up.' Judi stretched out her feet and surveyed the tips of her fluffy pink mules gloomily. 'I told Daddy tonight that I was staying at Inveray indefinitely. I must be mad!'

Fiona did not have to ask her the cause of her depression. Instead she said, 'Your uncle and aunt are very pleased that you're staying on. You're driving your uncle to Edinburgh next week, aren't you?'

'Yes. He's got to see the specialist again.' She brightened visibly. 'You and Jenny could come with us, couldn't you, Fiona? We could have fun . . . take Jenny to see the Castle! She'd like that, wouldn't she?'

'I'm sure she would! What a lovely plan, Judi!' Fiona exclaimed.

'You must buy her a kilt. I know a gorgeous shop in Princes Street! *And* I know somewhere where we can get a super lunch. I've been there before, with Rowan.'

'Oh?'

Judi looked at her. 'You know, I don't think you like Rowan very much! It's queer, when you used to be such pals when you were younger!'

'Oh, we've outgrown each other!' Fiona said lightly. 'We've nothing at all in common.'

'You like Bruce, though, don't you?'

'Yes. Yes, I do.'

Judi sighed. 'I suppose he *can* be quite nice—sometimes! But he isn't a patch on Rowan!'

'I wouldn't say that. He's a different type, that's all.'

'And yours, not mine!' Judi laughed, her good humour miraculously restored. 'I'm going to bed, you'll be glad to hear. 'Night, Fiona. Sleep well!'

Fiona was so tired that she did not think she would have much difficulty in doing exactly that, but she was proved wrong. For a long, long time sleep eluded her and when at last she did fall into an uneasy doze it was to dream, vividly and disjointedly, of tombstones and Rowan Macrae, sour apples and a girl with red hair. . . .

CHAPTER IV

Fiona spent the next few days revisiting old haunts and renewing old friendships. Everyone was delighted to welcome her back to the village and Jenny, in particular, had so much fuss made of her that Fiona laughingly protested that her head would be turned.

'Not much fear of that,' Margaret Campbell said. 'You've brought her up too well, Fiona.'

It was a compliment that Fiona treasured, since she was quite aware that as an 'only' child it would have been easy for Jenny to have become thoroughly spoilt. Margaret, she knew, would have been quick to spot any flaws in the child's upbringing and equally quick to point them out. (She didn't, it was true, care overmuch for Jenny's American accent, but admitted that in the circumstances it was probably inevitable.)

Jenny adored Inveray and everyone in it, including—much to Judi's surprised disapproval!—Bruce Buchanan. She spent a lot of time with him and also with her grandparents, but was happiest whenever Fiona and Judi joined forces and suggested a tramp across the hills and a picnic lunch. Fiona, who knew every inch of the countryside, found that Jenny would walk for miles, eager to explore the paths and caves and lochans that her mother had often told her about and to follow the busy streams which splashed and sparkled down the wooded hillsides in tiny silver cascades. Wandering amongst trees afire with the glow of dying leaves, she tried to make friends with the shy little roe deer in the woods, and through her grandfather's field glasses she watched the stately red deer on the hillside and learned to recognise the birds that had been only names to her before.

Judi seemed to enjoy these expeditions as much as mother and daughter, though sometimes she liked to pretend that her energy wasn't equal to theirs.

'Honestly, I haven't had so much exercise in *years*!' she proclaimed one afternoon, flinging herself down on the springy turf which was bright with sheets of purple heather and dotted here and there with dark peaty pools and patches of green moss. 'I'm sure I must have lost *pounds*, and I wasn't exactly overweight to start with!'

Fiona laughed. Like Judi she was wearing shorts and shirt and her arms and legs were brown and bare. 'I don't think you need worry too much! Have some chicken!' and she began unpacking the rucksack she had been carrying. 'We seem to have enough food here to feed an army!'

'Trust Aunt Margaret! She's used to healthy appetites!' Judi's dark eyes gleamed appreciatively as Fiona laid cold chicken, hardboiled eggs, salad, cheese, bread and chocolate out on the grass. It all looked very appetising and evidently Jenny thought so, too, for she gave a squeal of delight and asked if she could start.

'Of course.' Fiona took a piece of chicken herself but did not eat it immediately. This had been a favourite picnic spot for herself and Neil and Rowan. Just as she and Jenny and Judi were doing now they'd lain on the sun-warmed grass and laughed and talked and argued as they'd demolished the vast quantities of food prepared for them. Now Neil's laughter had been stilled for ever, and Rowan—

'Come back, Fiona!' It was Judi's voice which interrupted her thoughts. 'You're a hundred years away from us! Come back!'

'Not quite a hundred.' Fiona made herself answer lightly, angry with herself for a moment of weakness. She had not seen Rowan since the night he had come to dinner and she had made up her mind not to think about him or about the past any more than she could help. It could not serve any useful purpose—in fact, it could only do her harm.

Judi could be perceptive when she chose. 'You don't like remembering, do you? You looked so sad just then.'

Jenny heard her. She stopped eating and looked at her mother anxiously. Fiona saw the look and laughed almost convincingly.

'Nonsense! Who could be sad on a day like this? Look, there's not a cloud in the sky!'

'It's too good to last,' Judi said pessimistically. 'We've been lucky so far.' She took another piece of chicken, adding as she did so, 'You'll have to jog Rowan's memory about the launch, Fiona. It'd be a pity to wait until the weather breaks.'

'I haven't seen him since the other night.'

'Neither have I. I rang him up yesterday and he said he'd been frightfully busy. He's taking me out to dinner on Friday, though, so I suppose that's something to look forward to!'

'Of course. Where is he taking you?'

'He didn't say.' Judi gazed down at the distant loch, lying still and quiet among the wooded hills. 'You know, Aunt Margaret thinks I'm throwing myself at his head. I suppose I am, in a way, but—oh, Fiona, isn't it *hell* being in love? Can you remember? Or perhaps it was different for you—'

Fiona's cheeks burned. She said hurriedly, 'Oh, there are always problems! But I think you're probably worrying unnecessarily, Judi. I'm sure Rowan finds you extremely attractive. Any man would.'

Judi sighed. 'Sometimes I think I just amuse him. I've been told that the only thing he ever takes really seriously is his work, and I've got a horrible feeling that that's true. Women are light entertainment, and nothing else!'

Fiona thought of Tessa and in spite of the warmth of the day she shivered involuntarily. 'Don't let him break your heart, Judi.'

'I suppose that's on the cards.' Judi looked bleak for a moment, then she grinned. 'Still, it might make me a better actress if he did! The producer of the last play I was in—it folded after the first week, incidentally—informed me that I lacked emotional maturity! I thought it was rather beastly of him at the time, but I suppose he could be right!'

Fiona forbore to smile. She rather agreed with the unknown producer, but it wouldn't do to tell Judi so! Instead she said lightly, 'Well, I certainly can't see you as Lady Macbeth, but you might be quite good as Rosalind!'

Judi giggled. 'No fear! I'd hate to do Shakespeare! Bruce is quite right, you know. I *am* empty-headed!'

'Good heavens! Is that what he said?'

'Well, not in so many words, perhaps, but I always know what he's thinking!—Want some chocolate, Jenny, or another piece of chicken?'

Jenny plumped for chocolate. Fiona poured out coffee for herself and Judi and lemonade for her daughter and the talk became less personal. After they had all finished eating Fiona stowed the remains of the food away in the rucksack, then sat back and watched Judi and Jenny scramble among the rocks. Despite what the former said about exercise, she always seemed

61

to be bubbling over with excess energy!

'Come and join us, lazybones!' Judi, turning her head to call to Fiona, caught her toe on a stone, stumbled, tried desperately to save herself and fell awkwardly. When Fiona reached her she was white-faced and clutching at her right ankle.

'Oh, God, what a fool I am! Fiona, I'm sorry, I think I've done something to my beastly ankle!'

Fiona stared in dismay at the injured ankle, which was already beginning to look puffy and swollen.

'You certainly have! Oh, what rotten luck, Judi!' She knelt down to try to ascertain the nature of the injury and Judi winced with pain at her touch, gentle though it was. 'You poor thing! I'm pretty sure there's nothing broken, but it's quite a nasty sprain.'

Jenny's eyes were wide and anxious. 'How are you going to get home? Can you walk?'

'I shall have to hop or hobble,' Judi said, trying to laugh. 'You two will have to help me, though. I shan't be able to manage on my own!'

Fiona was looking worried. 'Don't think about that for a moment, sit down and rest. Jenny, take my hankie, please, and dip it into that little burn over there. The cold water may help to keep the swelling down.'

Jenny did as she was told. When she returned Fiona wrapped the wet handkerchief round Judi's ankle, now badly swollen, but though Judi assured her that the ice-cold water eased the pain it was obvious that she was in great discomfort. Fiona and Jenny helped her as much as they could, but her eventual journey down the mountainside was slow and agonisingly painful. By the time she reached the road she was as white as paper and gritting her teeth.

It was with relief that Fiona heard the sound of an

approaching car. The driver, a middle-aged farmer whom she knew slightly, grasped the situation immediately he saw the little group and was only too willing to help by giving them a lift back to Cragside.

'Best let the doctor have a look at that ankle,' he advised Judi. 'It's probably only a sprain, but you want to make sure that there's nothing broken.'

Margaret Campbell, too, thought this was good advice and telephoned Rowan almost immediately. When he arrived Fiona had no chance to make herself scarce and so was forced to become a reluctant onlooker.

'You silly child! What were you trying to do— climb a mountain in high-heeled shoes?' Rowan's words were teasing, but his smile, as he bent over his white-faced patient, brought an answering sparkle to her dark eyes.

'I'm not *that* stupid, Rowan Macrae!'

He laughed and ruffled her hair affectionately. 'Perhaps not! But I'm afraid the end result is just the same, my little one. It's a pretty nasty sprain and you're going to have to keep off it for the next few days —or else!'

Judi stared at him. 'But I'm supposed to be taking Uncle Douglas to Edinburgh on Thursday! He's got an appointment with the specialist!'

'Well, I agree that that's important, but *you* can't drive him, my dear.' Rowan's voice was firm. He glanced across at Margaret Campbell, who was looking anxious. 'I expect you can make other arrangements, can't you?'

'It's going to be rather difficult at this late date. Bruce can't take him, I know, he's got another engagement, and you don't drive, do you, Fiona?'

Fiona shook her head. 'No. I'm afraid I've never

learned.'

'H'm.' Rowan looked thoughtful. He was silent for a moment or two, then said with sudden decision, 'I'll take him. Yes, really!' as Margaret began to protest. 'It's all right. I've got one or two things to do in Edinburgh myself and it won't matter if I do them this week instead of next, as I'd planned.'

'Rowan, are you sure? It really would be most kind—' Margaret began, but Judi interrupted her.

'What about Fiona and Jenny? I was taking them as well. We'd promised Jenny that she'd see Edinburgh Castle!'

Rowan turned and looked at Fiona for the first time since he'd entered the room. There was no smile in his eyes for her, as there had been for Judi: they were cool and impersonal. She said hastily, before he could speak, 'Oh, as if that matters! We can always see the Castle another time, Judi.'

'But Jenny will be so terribly disappointed! She's been looking forward to it so much, and you know what children are!' Judi said, looking really distressed.

'Judi, don't be silly! She's not a baby, she'll understand—'

'I don't quite know what the fuss is about.' Rowan's quiet, slow voice was almost a drawl. 'Naturally I shall be delighted if Fiona and Jenny will accept a lift with me. There's plenty of room in the car.'

'Thank you, but I wouldn't dream of troubling you!' Fiona, furious at being placed in such an embarrassing situation, spoke angrily.

Rowan's eyes met hers and this time they held a familiar gleam. 'No trouble at all, I assure you.'

'But—' Fiona stopped, biting her lip. If she persisted in her objections she would merely succeed in making herself look absurd. And Jenny would be disappointed if the trip had to be postponed, of course she would. If only anyone but Rowan had been involved. . . .

Judi was obviously puzzled by her reaction. 'I only wish I could come as well! Trouble is, I don't fancy the idea of hobbling down the length of Princes Street!'

'I'll bring you back a present for being a good girl,' Rowan told her. 'What would you like?'

Judi's eyes sparkled. 'Surprise me!'

Fiona turned away, her lips tightly compressed. If Judi was in fact throwing herself at Rowan's head he seemed to be doing absolutely nothing to discourage her. Quite the reverse. Perhaps he really was falling in love with her . . . and even if he wasn't he would never dare to treat her as callously as he had treated Tessa MacGregor. Poor Tessa had had nobody to fight for her or to care what happened to her. Rowan had been lucky, Fiona thought bitterly. She had let her father disown her rather than involve her lover in a scandal which would surely have broken old Dr Macrae's heart. He'd been so proud of his clever, handsome son.

Staring out of the window while Rowan bandaged Judi's ankle, Fiona found herself wondering how Rowan had ever become attracted by Tessa and how, in a small clachan, they had managed to keep their liaison such a close secret. Even when Tessa's condition had become known it seemed that no one had dreamed that Rowan might be responsible. And he had kept quiet and allowed the girl he had loved to suffer alone and unaided. It was that that Fiona found impossible to forgive. Not the liaison itself.

She found herself remembering what Neil had said. Manlike, he'd tried hard to find excuses for his friend's behaviour.

' He's behaved very badly, Fiona, but Tessa is beautiful enough to turn anyone's head . . . even Rowan's!'
he'd said. And then, ' Try not to judge him too
harshly.'

Recalling those words, Fiona checked a sigh. She
was, in effect, still doing that and she had no right to
do so. Whatever had passed between Rowan and
Tessa was now ancient history and a matter for his own
conscience. She could never forget the way he had
behaved, but she was no longer a romantic, idealistic
teenager and Rowan was no longer the parfit gentil
knight of her dreams. They had both grown up, painfully in her own case and perhaps—judging by that
bitter little twist to his mouth—in Rowan's also.

' Well, Fiona? Am I to look forward to the pleasure
of your company on Thursday?' Rowan had walked
to the door and halted there to address her across the
room.

' Thank you. If you're quite sure that Jenny and I
won't be in the way—'

' You won't.' His smile softened his whole face,
made Fiona suddenly realise that he could, if he chose,
exercise a dangerous charm. Small wonder that Judi
was in danger of losing her head over him and that in
comparison Bruce Buchanan seemed to her to be dull
and uninteresting! Only of course she, Fiona, was
quite unsusceptible. She was as indifferent to Rowan
as he was to her, which was why it was so silly, she told
herself impatiently, to feel so emotionally tensed every
time she came into contact with him.

When Thursday arrived she and Jenny were ready
and waiting in the hall as Rowan's car drew up beside
the front door. Jenny was wearing her favourite coat
—navy-blue with white piping—and her small vivid

face was flushed with excitement. Nobody seemed to notice that her enthusiasm for the trip was not being shared by her mother—nobody except, perhaps, Rowan.

'I'd ask you to sit in the front, Fiona, if I weren't perfectly sure you'd much rather sit in the back with Jenny,' he said coolly, opening the car door for her as he spoke.

'Thank you.' Fiona was relieved that the presence of her father-in-law would probably make it unnecessary for her and Rowan to exchange more than a few odd remarks. It wasn't so much what he said, as the way he said it, that made her suspect that he guessed how ill at ease she felt in his company. And that it gave him a queer, perverse satisfaction. . . .

The journey to Edinburgh was rather a silent one. Jenny, who was still a little in awe of the 'doctor man', as she called Rowan, was content to sit with her button nose pressed against the car window, watching the countryside flash by. Neither Rowan nor his front seat passenger seemed to be in a talkative mood so that Fiona, much to her relief, was able to lose herself in her own thoughts. She had received two letters that morning from the States. One was from her great friend and next-door neighbour, Lissa Denton. The other was from Stephen Connaught. Steve, the man whom before she'd left for England she'd almost promised to marry. Wealthy, distinguished, *reliable* Steve. . . .

He hadn't wanted her to make the trip. Had urged her not to. 'I hope, Fiona, that you're going to miss me as much as I feel sure that I'm going to miss you,' he'd told her the night before she went away. 'If you do, perhaps when you come back . . .' He'd left his sentence unfinished, but Fiona had known what was in his mind. Dear Steve, who was always so kind and helpful . . . why couldn't she make up her mind to marry him? Lissa had so often told her that that was what she ought to do.

'For heaven's sake, honey, what's holding you back? You're fond of the guy, aren't you, and it's obvious he thinks the world of you!' she'd exclaimed in honest bewilderment. And Fiona, who really was fond of Steve, had found it quite impossible to explain that the bitterness of her first marriage had made her distinctly wary of taking on any other commitments. Whatever he said now Stephen, like Neil, might expect more—far more—than the loyalty and affection which was all she had to give. Everything else belonged to Jenny.

Staring at the back of Rowan's dark, well-shaped head, Fiona suddenly found herself thinking of Judi's despairing 'Oh, Fiona, isn't it *hell* being in love?' What would the younger girl have said, she wondered bleakly, if she'd told her that it was because of what Rowan had done to her that she'd never been able to trust her heart again? He'd done something to her, that day by the loch. Destroyed a part of her so completely that it had never ever had a chance to grow again.

'Poor Judi. It's a shame she's missing this trip.' Douglas Campbell turned his head and smiled at his daughter-in-law. She was too quiet, he reflected. Was she perhaps bored by the prospect before her? Jenny wouldn't be satisfied until she'd seen the Castle, and of course Fiona had seen it all before. The thought made him add, 'You'd have enjoyed her company too, wouldn't you? I'm afraid I shan't be much use to you, my dear: after I've seen the specialist I'm lunching with my lawyer, who's an old friend. We shall probably spend most of the afternoon going through my affairs.'

'Oh, don't worry about us!' Fiona assured him. 'Jenny and I will find plenty to do, won't we, poppet?'

'I hope you'll do me the honour of joining me for lunch?' Rowan spoke pleasantly, but there was a note in his voice which warned Fiona that he would not readily take 'No' for an answer. Nevertheless, she demurred.

'I don't really think we shall want a proper lunch ... just a cup of coffee and some sandwiches at a snack bar. Besides, you said you had things to do, Rowan. I'm sure you won't want to be bothered with us.'

'One, my business won't take very long and two, of course you'll want a proper lunch.' Rowan, halting the car at an intersection, turned his head and smiled at Jenny. 'I know a restaurant where they serve the most delicious chocolate icecream you've ever tasted. Wouldn't you rather have that, and perhaps chicken or roast beef beforehand, than the couple of cheese sandwiches that your mother seems to think will satisfy a growing girl's appetite?'

It was the smile, and not the promise of the icecream, that made a traitor of Jenny. 'Much rather!' she agreed solemnly.

'Then that's settled.' Rowan transferred his attention back to the road. 'I'll meet you at one o'clock, Fiona, by the Scott Monument in Princes Street Gardens.'

He had got it all mapped out, Fiona thought resentfully. His bland assumption that she would be willing to fall in with his plans infuriated her, but she bit back the words which trembled on her lips. Perhaps he saw her expression in his driving mirror, for he suddenly laughed.

'Were you always so prickly and independent, Fiona, or have you changed?'

Fiona didn't answer. There was no point. This round to Rowan, she thought wryly, and then, ' Oh, if only Judi were here!'

On arriving in Edinburgh Rowan parked the car and they all went their different ways. Rowan insisted on escorting Douglas Campbell to the hospital where he had an appointment with a famous eye specialist and Fiona and Jenny made straight for the Castle, brooding on its rocky site overlooking the heart of the city. The time flew by as they wandered round the gorgeous apartments steeped in history, and it was with a shock of real dismay that Fiona, glancing at her watch, suddenly realised that it was nearly one o'clock. Reluctant though she was to lunch with Rowan she had not intended to keep him waiting, so that when she and Jenny eventually arrived at the Scott Memorial, very much out of breath and nearly twenty minutes late, her apology was perfectly genuine.

' . . . so of course we've simply *rushed*! Have you been waiting long?' she asked breathlessly.

' Since ten to one, but not to worry, since you've arrived at last.' Rowan gave her a slightly malicious grin. ' You were so reluctant to accept my invitation that I must admit I was beginning to wonder if you'd deliberately stood me up!'

Fiona gave an embarrassed little laugh. ' As if I would! H-have you done all the things that you wanted to do?'

' Apart from finding something to console Judi, yes. Any suggestions?' Rowan asked as they walked down Princes Street.

' I'm sure she'd much rather that you did the choosing.'

'Oh? I wouldn't have thought that it mattered. Anyway, it can certainly wait until this afternoon.—In here, Fiona,' and Rowan, catching hold of Jenny with one hand and cupping Fiona's elbow with the other, piloted them into a big, beautifully appointed restaurant where the tables were set back in alcoves, lit softly by wall lights.

The meal with which they were served was superb and Rowan made a most pleasant and attractive host. At least Jenny obviously thought so. Fiona, watching the way that he was charming her small daughter, felt a prickle of dismay and was immediately annoyed with herself. Perhaps Rowan genuinely liked children . . . all children. He certainly had a way with them.

The waiter came hovering, his face split with a smile. 'Would your daughter like more icecream, sir?—It is good, yes?' to Jenny, who was blissfully licking her last spoonful.

Fiona blushed vividly, but Rowan, instead of correcting the man's mistake, said easily, 'I'm sure she would like some more. I told you it was delicious, didn't I, Jenny?'

Jenny nodded vigorously. Rowan waited until another bowl of icecream had engaged her attention and then turned to Fiona. For the first time that day his dark blue eyes were lit by a gleam of the mockery she found so distasteful.

'Why did you look so embarrassed simply because the waiter, poor man, made a perfectly natural assumption?' Then, as she made no reply, 'After all, you and I might well have had a daughter one day if Neil hadn't somehow or another made you suddenly realise how much more he had to offer you than I!'

A spoon clattered out of Fiona's hand. 'That isn't true! I—' She stopped dead, realising too late the trap she had fallen into. She saw his brows lift ironically and added angrily, 'I—I do wish you wouldn't keep on harking back to the past! It's—it's so futile!'

'Very true.' Rowan leaned back in his chair. His eyes held hers for a long moment and something in the quality of his gaze set a little pulse beating in her throat. 'However, I wasn't harking back, as you call it. I was merely trying to point out that your embarrassment was misplaced.'

Fiona was saved from answering by Jenny, who was smiling radiantly at her benefactor. 'That was the best icecream I've ever tasted! Thank you very much for a lovely lunch, Dr Macrae.'

Rowan surveyed her gravely. 'Don't you think that as your mother and I are such old friends "Dr Macrae" is a little too formal?'

Jenny considered, her eyes sparkling. 'Could I call you "Uncle", do you think? I've only got one and that's Uncle Steve, back in the States.'

'Uncle Steve?'

'Yes. He's a great friend of Mommy's—'

Fiona cut her short. 'He's a publisher. I illustrate some of his children's books for him,' she said crisply.

Jenny obviously felt a need to elaborate. 'He's nice,' she told Rowan. 'But he's got grey hair. I heard Auntie Lissa tell someone that he'll probably marry Mommy one day, but I hope he won't. He's quite old, you see.'

'Jenny!' Fiona exclaimed, but Rowan threw back his head and laughed.

'Don't be cross with her, Fiona! I'd have thought that her opinions might interest you!' he said sardonically. Then, as she bit her lip, 'Incidentally, how old is "quite old"? Fifty? Sixty?'

'Steve happens to be in his early forties. He does

72

have grey hair, but the effect is very distinguished.'
Fiona rose to her feet. 'Thank you for inviting us to
lunch, Rowan. I've enjoyed it.'

'Don't speak with such a distressing air of finality!
I was hoping to inflict my presence upon you for the
rest of the afternoon.' He smiled at Jenny. 'Perhaps
you could help me to choose a present for Judi. I'm
afraid I seem to have run out of good ideas.'

'Oh, we'll help, won't we, Mommy?' Jenny said
eagerly, and Fiona, meeting Rowan's quizzical eyes,
laughed reluctantly. He knew how to get his own way.
He always had.

'That's better!' Rowan regarded her approvingly.
'You should laugh much more often, Fiona. I was
beginning to think that perhaps you'd forgotten how.'
He paused and added softly, 'Among all the other
things you seem to have forgotten.'

It was easier—and safer—to pretend that she had
not heard him. She bent over Jenny, helping her to
button her coat. When she again looked up Rowan
was smiling a little oddly.

'I'm glad you had a daughter, Fiona.'

She didn't ask him why. 'I'm glad, too.' She
brushed back her hair from her eyes. 'If you're
ready—'

Rowan. paid the bill and led the way out of the
restaurant into the sunlit splendour of Princes Street.
He seemed to be in the gayest of moods and Fiona,
listening to the way he laughed and joked with Jenny,
felt her throat suddenly tighten. What a fascinating
person he could be when, as now, he dropped his mask
of smiling cynicism! If, of course, it really was a mask.

At any rate, it was impossible to remain wary and
defensive when the other two were so obviously determined to enjoy themselves! She found herself un-

73

bending, her misgivings regarding Rowan evaporating. How silly to be afraid of him! How could he possibly do anything to hurt her now? She was no longer an emotional nineteen-year-old, dazzled into believing that a teenager's infatuation was something real and lasting. She was a mature woman, mother of a child, and Rowan was merely someone she had known a long, long time ago. Why remember the heartbreak he'd caused her? There just wasn't any point. . . .

In the end they left the buying of Judi's present until the very last moment, and then it was Jenny who chose it—an exquisite (and shockingly expensive) little model of a galloping horse in blue-green china.

'It's the nicest thing in the shop,' she said with conviction.

'Right. Then if there's another just like it you shall have it,' Rowan told her.

Jenny's eyes widened and she flushed. '*Me?* But—' She looked anxiously at her mother, who had opened her lips to utter an instinctive protest.

Rowan forestalled her. 'Your mother won't mind. Uncles are always allowed to buy presents for their nieces,' he said firmly.

'Judi's not your niece,' Jenny pointed out.

'Well, no. Not exactly,' Rowan conceded, laughing. He picked up a bottle containing a beautifully made little sailing ship. 'While I'm about it I'll buy one of these. I think I know someone who'd like it.'

'Who?' Jenny asked curiously. 'You haven't got any children of your own, have you?'

'Heaven forbid!' Rowan said, laughing, and Fiona stiffened in spite of herself.

For a brief moment her eyes met Rowan's and she saw his smile fade, almost as though he could read her thoughts. With that one casual remark he had dis-

74

pelled the magic of the afternoon and the old bitterness returned in full force.

It was no good, she thought drearily, turning away to pick up a piece of bric-a-brac with fingers that shook a little. She'd never be able to forget Tessa, or forgive Rowan for what he had done.

CHAPTER V

A couple of days after the Edinburgh excursion Rowan telephoned Fiona to tell her that his father had been asking when she intended to pay him a visit.

'I hope you'll be able to make it some time this week? He's really looking forward to seeing you, Fiona, you were always a favourite of his.'

'Oh, Rowan! It isn't that I haven't thought about him! But everyone said how ill he'd been—'

'He's a lot better now. He still isn't strong enough to enjoy a lot of visitors, but I think half an hour with you might do him a lot of good.'

'Do you think I should bring Jenny?'

Rowan hesitated. 'Perhaps not, the first time. Unless you'd rather not leave her behind?'

'Her grandmother is taking her out to tea with some friends on Thursday. If that day's all right for your father—?'

'Fine. I'll come and fetch you at half-past three,' Rowan said briskly, and rang off before Fiona could protest that there was no need, she could easily walk.

She was frowning a little when she rejoined Judi, who was still unable to do much more than hobble about on her injured ankle. She chafed constantly against her enforced inactivity, though everyone tried hard to amuse and entertain her. Even Bruce had brought her some magazines, though Judi seemed amused at his choice of reading matter.

'You'd have thought he'd have tried to find something a little more scintillating than "The Countryman" and "Country Life", wouldn't you?' she said to Fiona, flicking the pages over with an idle finger. 'He

76

has no imagination at all, and that's his trouble!'

'*I* think it was very kind of him to bother! What an ungrateful brat you are at times!' Fiona said, laughing.

Judi gave her a slightly shamefaced grin. 'I suppose I am. But at least I didn't let on to Bruce that I'd rather have had something light and entirely frivolous! In fact, I was extraordinarily nice to him, with the result that he stayed for the best part of half an hour and only looked at his watch once! Such condescension! I could hardly believe it!'

'You're not fair to Bruce. He works terribly hard and puts in some frightfully long hours. Uncle says he simply doesn't know what he'd do without him.'

Judi opened her dark eyes wide. 'But, darling Fiona, that's just the *point*! Nobody—but nobody! —ought to be that conscientious! Life's for living, after all, not just *working*!'

'A man's work is tremendously important to him.' Fiona hesitated, then added, 'Rowan is just as dedicated to his, in his own way.'

'Yes, but he doesn't prose about it all the time!' Judi retorted. 'Not that I'd really mind if he did— medicine is so much more interesting than agriculture!'

'I don't agree—' Fiona began, but was interrupted by Judi's mischievous chuckle.

'That's because you aren't particularly interested in Rowan himself! In fact, you almost seem to go out of your way to avoid him. It's funny, when you liked him so much in the old days.'

Fiona's hands clenched, but she forced herself to answer casually. 'I think he's a bit too sure of himself and a bit too ruthless. That cynicism of his repels me. He used not to be like that.'

'I think it's a sort of protective armour, you know.

77

Someone told me—oh, ages ago!—that he took a fearful toss over some woman. I don't know all the details and of course he never talks about it, but nevertheless I'm pretty sure it's true.'

If it was, Fiona thought bleakly, Rowan had got no more than his just deserts. *She* certainly wasn't going to waste any sympathy on him!

Her own daughter, she was dismayed to find, was definitely to be counted as another of Rowan's conquests. She talked about him continually and the little china horse he had given her was her most prized possession.

'It cost far too much money and of course you shouldn't have bought it for her, but she really does adore it,' Fiona told Rowan when he came to collect her on Thursday. 'She has quite a thing about horses, you know. Bruce has promised to teach her to ride when he has a few moments to spare and she's thrilled to bits at the prospect.'

'Why don't you teach her?' Rowan asked.

Fiona coloured faintly. 'I haven't been on horseback for years.'

'Pity. You used to be darned good.' Rowan turned his head and smiled at her. 'Remember our pony-trekking expeditions? We used to have some marvellous times, didn't we?'

Fiona tensed. She didn't want to talk about the past. It was too full of bitter-sweet memories which, even now, had the power to hurt. She said briefly 'Yes' and followed up the monosyllable with a random question.

'Is Mrs Brady still your father's housekeeper?' Rowan, like Fiona herself, had been motherless from an early age and this at one time had been another bond between them.

'She is, but I'm afraid the job is becoming a little too much for her, especially since Father's illness.' Rowan paused, then added deliberately, 'It's a great disappointment to her that I haven't yet married. I rather suspect that she's made up her mind to abdicate for my wife and for no one else.'

Fiona smiled brilliantly. 'At least she must live in perpetual hope! I've heard quite a lot about your conquests, Rowan.'

Her voice was laced with sarcasm and Rowan was quick to respond in kind. When he next spoke his old mocking challenge was back in command.

'Since when have you listened to local gossip, Fiona?'

She countered his question with another. 'Can one avoid listening to it in a small community like this?'

'Possibly not, but there's no need to take it too seriously. My conquests, as you are pleased to call them, haven't been that thick on the ground.' He paused and added lightly, 'I've only been in love once in my life—really in love, that is—and that was such a painful and unpleasant experience that I've been in no hurry to repeat it.'

So Judi had been right! 'He took a fearful toss over some woman. . . .' The biter bit, with a vengeance!

She drew a deep breath and said coolly, 'That, of course, is the kind of remark intended to make all nice, tender-hearted girls feel sorry for you!'

There was a moment's silence. Then Rowan said, 'Meaning, I suppose, that you aren't a nice, tender-hearted girl and that you don't feel sorry for me?'

'If you like.' Fiona wished that she felt as cool and confident as she tried to appear. She added a little rashly, 'Don't forget that I'm not an ingénue like

79

Judi!'

'Ah, Judi.' Rowan's smile was speculative, tinged with mockery. 'You don't approve of our friendship, do you? I wonder why?'

'Because I like her and I don't want to see her get hurt,' Fiona said bluntly. And then, 'Of course, if you really are serious about her——'

Rowan had stopped smiling. 'Even if I'm not, I'm not in the habit of hurting people. I haven't changed that much, Fiona, even if it is eight years since we last met.'

She knew if she answered him she might say too much. Rage gusted through her, but she sat silent, her hands clasped tightly in her lap. Rowan shot her one swift, bleak glance, then stared straight ahead of him with a strange tense expression round his mouth as he drove faster and faster.

For the rest of the journey there was a rather grim silence. Several times Fiona thought of breaking it, but though she searched desperately in her mind for a safe topic of conversation nothing presented itself. She found herself wishing that she had, after all, brought Jenny with her. If she had this strange tension wouldn't have existed and she and Rowan might have been on the same easy, friendly footing that they had been on that day in Edinburgh.

She was glad when at last Rowan turned the car through big iron gates set in a long stone wall. A short curving drive led to Rivendell, the Macraes' pleasant, rambling old house which was veiled with ivy and Virginia creeper and despite herself Fiona leant forward, her eyes eager. She had always loved Rivendell, which at one time had been almost a second home to her. It had had a hospitable, friendly atmosphere which both Cragside and the manse had lacked, and she had always been sure of a warm welcome. Dr Macrae, cheerful and kind-hearted, had been fond of all children and he had had a specially soft spot for Fiona.

Two collie puppies came rushing round the side of the house as the car stopped, and began barking excitedly. Fiona laughed and turned to Rowan.

'A traditional Rivendell welcome! But what's happened to dear old Rusty, Rowan?'

'She died last year, I'm afraid. These are two of her grandchildren,' Rowan said, caressing one silky head with lean brown fingers.

'What do you call them?'

'Castor and Pollux.' Rowan laughed at her expression. 'Mrs Brady named them. It had nothing to do with me!'

'What didn't?' demanded a brisk voice, and Fiona looked up to see Mrs Brady beaming at them from the doorway.

'Mrs Brady!' Fiona went up to her and gave her a quick hug, then bent and kissed the rosy cheek. 'Oh, it's lovely to see you again!'

It was Rowan who cut short the housekeeper's delighted and vociferous welcome.

'Where's Dad, Mrs Brady?'

'In the rose garden.' She smiled at Fiona and unashamedly wiped the tears from her eyes. 'Eh, but this is just like old times! You and Master Rowan—'

'Not quite like old times!' Fiona spoke hastily. She was uncomfortably aware that Mrs Brady had once entertained the hope that she and Rowan would marry and that the fact that her choice had fallen on Neil had been one of the housekeeper's most grievous disappointments. If she still had any ideas in that direction then the sooner they were discouraged the better!

Perhaps Rowan guessed what she was thinking, for his eyes gleamed, though he said nothing. Instead he led her round the house to find his father, who was carefully snipping off the heads of some late, dead roses. It hurt Fiona to see how slowly he moved and how pale and thin he looked, but though physically he was but a shadow of his former self nothing had detracted from the warmth of his personality or the kindness of his smile. His quiet 'Welcome home, Fiona' made her remember on how many occasions in the past she had had cause to be grateful for his understanding—something which her own father, good man though he had been, had lacked in no small measure. Only once had she ever failed to consult him on a matter of importance, and that was her marriage to Neil. Perhaps, if anyone but his own adored son had been involved in her heartbreak. . . . She thrust the thought from her hurriedly and forced herself to respond to the old man's greeting with the animation that she thought would be expected of her.

'Well, well, I must say that it's high time you came back to us, my dear!' Later, settling himself beside Fiona in his big, book-lined study while Mrs Brady bustled around laying a small table for tea, Dr Macrae regarded her with smiling approval. 'We've all missed you, and been sorry that America seemed to have secured such a firm hold on your affections! You really are planning to return there before so very long?'

'I—I must. I have a job, and friends who are expecting me—' Fiona stopped short, the blood creeping into her cheeks as she realised that Rowan was looking at her with a glint of teasing amusement. Of course he was remembering what Jenny had told him about Steve! He was probably thinking that she was anxious to get back to him!

'I'm sorry. We should very much like to have you and your daughter as permanencies in Inveray, Fiona, and of course it would mean a tremendous lot to your in-laws.' Dr Macrae stroked the big white cat which had jumped on to his knee and was purring loudly. 'You must tell me all about Jenny, though I've already heard a great deal from Rowan. I want you to promise that you'll bring her to see me as soon as you can spare the time for another visit, my dear.'

Fiona stretched out her hands to the blazing fire which took the chill out of the autumn afternoon. Here in Inveray no one, as yet, had central heating and in a way she could not help feeling glad.

'I'd like to do that if you're quite sure that the two of us wouldn't tire you too much?'

'Bless you, no! This tyrant'—he looked affectionately at his tall son, leaning against the mantelpiece— 'would deprive me of even the most innocent pleasures if he could! If that's the way he treats all his patients I'm surprised he hasn't been kicked out of the medical profession years ago!'

'Don't listen to him, Fiona. The strong-arm measures exist only in his imagination, I assure you,' Rowan said, smiling.

His father snorted. 'I imagine Fiona knows you well enough to believe you capable of almost anything in order to achieve your own ends!' he said darkly.

'Indeed I do.'

Rowan's mouth went down at one corner. If Dr Macrae had been joking, Fiona was obviously not.

'Since you both have such a low opinion of my character I don't suppose either of you will shed any tears if I beg to be excused for half an hour or so,' he said lightly. 'I've a patient in the glen I meant to visit this morning, only I didn't have time. Mrs Mac-Ian, who's expecting her sixth child, Father.'

Dr Macrae groaned. 'Another little MacIan who'll doubtless grow up to plague every gamekeeper within a radius of twenty miles! Born poachers, every one of them!'

'It may be a girl this time,' Fiona protested laughing.

Dr Macrae shook his head. 'No. It will be another boy. The MacIans have no use for daughters!'

'Well, we shall see.' Rowan moved towards the door with the assurance that was so common to him. 'I'll be back in time to give you a lift home, of course, Fiona.'

There was a little silence after his departure. Then Mrs Brady brought in the tea and Dr Macrae turned smilingly to Fiona.

'Will you do the honours, my dear?'

'Of course.' Fiona was amused and rather touched to discover that the housekeeper had seen fit to bring out the best silver teapot and the best Royal Worcester china in her honour. It seemed a far cry from the days when she and Rowan, muddy, dishevelled and usually starving, had been in the habit of rushing into the big, red-tiled kitchen and begging Mrs Brady for newly-baked cakes and scones to take out with them on to the moors.

'Penny for your thoughts, Fiona?'

One did not prevaricate with a man as shrewd as old Dr Macrae. 'I—I was just thinking of the way things used to be. In the old days.'

He regarded her whimsically. 'You and Rowan had a good friendship, my dear. To be frank, I was selfishly sorry when in the end it was Neil who managed to capture your heart. I thought at one time that you and Rowan—' He sighed and did not go on.

The colour flooded Fiona's cheeks and she did not answer.

'Now I've embarrassed you! I'm sorry. Shall we say that I should dearly have loved to have had you as a daughter and leave it at that?'

'It's a lovely compliment. Thank you.'

'You're a very lovely young woman.' Dr Macrae spoke with intentional lightness, annoyed with himself for having let his tongue run away with him. His pleasure at seeing Fiona after so many years had obviously made him less tactful than usual, he thought wryly. He leant back in his chair.

'Rowan tells me that Jenny is the spitting image of you at the same age. Has she also your propensity for getting into scrapes?'

Fiona laughed, relieved that the conversation had taken a safer turn. 'I don't think so. She's really very little trouble at all.'

She went on to talk of Jenny and their life in America and her host listened with sympathetic interest. He was laughing at something she had said when the sound of car wheels on the gravel outside told them that Rowan had returned.

'By exercising enormous self-control we've left you some food, but I'm afraid the tea is stone cold. Could you ask Mrs Brady to make you some more?' Fiona looked up as he entered the room.

'I've had some already, thanks. Mrs MacIan makes good tea, though the cup and saucer she gave me would have given Mrs Brady the horrors.'

'You'll survive,' his father said philosophically. 'And you're right. Betsy MacIan can't cook, but she does make good tea.'

'No sign yet of the expected addition to the family?' Fiona asked.

' No. He's not due for another four or five days, anyway.'

' Oh. Isn't she?' Fiona said provocatively, and Rowan grinned.

' We'll have a bet on it, if you like, Fiona.'

' We won't. You never lose,' Fiona said with feeling.

' There always has to be a first time.' He glanced at his watch. ' If you don't mind waiting just a moment while I make a telephone call, Fiona, I'll take you home. No, of course I'm not going to let you walk!' as she demurred.

' He's a good boy,' Dr Macrae said quietly as his son disappeared into the hall. ' Has anyone told you that he turned down a consultancy at one of the best hospitals in Edinburgh to help me out by taking over this practice?'

Fiona's eyes widened. ' I knew he'd turned down a good job, but I hadn't realised it was a consultancy. Isn't he frightfully young to be offered a post like that?'

' Yes. It was a great chance. I wish to goodness I'd known what he was going to do. I'd never have let him make such a sacrifice. He didn't say a word to me about it, you know. It was a colleague who told me, and Rowan was furious with him.'

' Yes. He would have been.' Fiona was conscious of a familiar little ache in her heart. Once she would have staked everything she owned on Rowan's integrity and loyalty, at all times. Poor Tessa!

Rowan came back into the study, Fiona's coat over his arm. He held it out for her and she slipped into it. For a moment his hands rested on her shoulders and his touch so unnerved her that she felt angry with herself. Why, after all this time and when he meant absolutely nothing to her, did Rowan's nearness affect her so strangely? She was fond of Steve Connaught

86

and enjoyed his company, yet on the one or two occasions that he had kissed her she had been completely unmoved. It simply wasn't fair.

In the car on the way back to Cragside they did not talk much and what little conversation there was centred round Dr Macrae.

'He wants me to bring Jenny to see him. I said I would, perhaps next week,' and Fiona looked at Rowan for agreement.

'Yes, I think that's a good idea. Incidentally, Fiona, Judi reminded me yesterday that I'd promised Jenny a trip in my launch. She seems keen on organising a picnic, though I'm not at all sure that it's picnic weather and it certainly won't be if we delay much longer. Are you free on Sunday?'

'I—yes, I think so.'

'Then perhaps you'd be kind enough to tell her to go ahead with the arrangements. I've suggested that she might invite Buchanan, if he's free. Four adults will be better than three and I've noticed that you seem to enjoy his company.'

Fiona flushed. Of course, what he meant was that he hoped that Bruce would take care of her so that he could devote most of his own attention to Judi! Well, that was all right by her.

Coldly she said, 'Full marks for your observation. I do.'

'He's your type. Worthy, conscientious and serious-minded.' Rowan sent her an amused, sideways look as he stopped the car outside the house. Sitting there, relaxed and handsome at the wheel, his dark wavy hair glistening in the late afternoon sun, he looked very much master of the situation. His bland self-confidence so infuriated Fiona that she got out of the car without waiting for him to open the door for her, but she could not resist the temptation to say crossly, ' I should be interested to know what makes you think that those three qualities particularly appeal to me!'

Rowan glanced at her with a lifted brow and his mouth curved. ' I'd have thought that was obvious. The fact that I, alas! lack them all,' he said softly, and let in the clutch. ' Goodbye, Fiona. Thanks for coming.'

The car disappeared down the drive in a small cloud of dust. For a moment Fiona stood staring after it, then almost angrily she turned aside. The front door opened as she ran up the wide shallow steps that led to it and Bruce Buchanan came out. He seemed lost in thought, but he smiled when he saw Fiona.

' Hello. Enjoyed your visit?'

' Yes. Who told you where I'd been?'

' Judi. I think she'd have liked to have gone with you.' Bruce stuck his hands in the pockets of his ancient sports jacket and added wryly, ' I thought I'd keep her company for a few minutes, but I'm sorry I bothered. She left me in no doubt whatsoever that as far as she's concerned I'm a very poor substitute for Rowan Macrae!'

Judi really *was* a brat at times, Fiona thought indignantly. Aloud she said hesitantly, ' Inactivity makes her irritable. I know she can be frightfully difficult, but—but she's sound at the core, you know.'

Of all the pompous speeches! she reflected ruefully. Rowan, no doubt, would have blistered her with a scathing rejoinder, but Bruce merely smiled, though his eyes weren't amused.

' I do know,' he said, and something in his voice made Fiona think, ' *Heavens!* He's in love with her!'

For a second or two the surprise of her discovery rendered her speechless, then she pulled herself together. Bruce would not thank her for letting him know that she had guessed his secret.

'Is Jenny home yet, do you know? She's been out to tea with her grandmother.'

'I don't think she is, but you'll find Judi in the library, listening to records. Mind she doesn't either deafen you or drive you to suicide!'

Fiona understood the meaning of this cryptic remark a few moments later. Judi, her face moody, was curled up in the depths of a big leather armchair, looking smaller and more waif-like than ever. The radiogram was on and a deafening flood of music filled the room. Fiona had no difficulty in recognising what it was. 'Dream of the Witches' Sabbath'.

Her lips twitched in spite of herself. Poor Bruce! Judi had certainly found a subtle way of indicating that his presence was unwelcome. Demon-haunted forests, with ghosts and goblins closing in from all sides, weren't exactly to everybody's taste.

She had to raise her voice to make herself heard above the music. 'Heavens, Judi! Is this your idea of pleasant entertainment?'

Judi grinned reluctantly, got up and removed the record. 'Sorry. I couldn't get rid of Bruce so I suggested listening to records. I think he rather expected something light and frothy, so I took great pleasure in surprising him!'

'I didn't know Uncle was an admirer of Hector Berlioz!'

'I don't suppose he is. It's an old record: probably one of Neil's.' Judi returned to her chair. 'Well, how did you find Rowan's father?'

'Surprisingly well, all things considered, and very cheerful.'

Judi traced a pattern with her forefinger on the arm

89

of her chair. 'He doesn't see many people. You're obviously one of the privileged few, Fiona.'

'Well, we've known each other quite a long time,' Fiona pointed out lightly.

'I suppose so. Did Rowan bring you home? I didn't hear the car.' Then, as Fiona nodded, 'Why didn't he come in?'

She sounded all at once very young.

'I didn't ask him, and anyway, I don't suppose he'd have had time. He's got surgery this evening.' Fiona hesitated, then added, 'He mentioned a picnic on Sunday, said would I ask you to go ahead with the necessary arrangements. I rather gathered that he wants you to invite Bruce.'

'Yes, he does, but I don't know whether his lordship will come. I've an idea he won't care for such frivolities!'

'He may surprise you,' Fiona suggested, and then, as Judi snorted, smiled a little ruefully. Judi obviously had no idea that Bruce was smitten with her charms and probably wouldn't believe it if she was told. She was nothing if not single-minded and at present it was Rowan who occupied her thoughts to the exclusion of everyone else.

CHAPTER VI

Though dark clouds on Saturday threatened a break in the golden weather, Sunday proved to be an ideal day for a picnic . . . a day of breeze and blue, warm and sunny.

'Thank heaven for St Luke's little summer!' Fiona thought, smiling at Jenny's excitement as she helped her mother and Judi to pack the hamper for their lunch. Smoked salmon, fried chicken, ham and tongue, crusty new bread rolls . . . well, at least they wouldn't starve!

'What about drinks?' she asked Judi.

'Rowan said to leave that to him. I hope he'll think of something nice!'

Just at that moment Bruce arrived to drive them down to the loch, where Rowan was already waiting alongside the slip. The water was a smooth unbroken stretch, gleaming silver in the sun, dark with reflections near the shore, and Jenny gave a little gasp of delight as they all crowded on to the trim, freshly-painted launch.

'It's a bonnie, bonnie boat, Uncle Rowan!'

'Thank you,' Rowan said gravely, and Fiona met his eyes and laughed.

'An improvement, don't you think? Two weeks ago it would have been a " super " or a " smashing " boat!' she said.

'We'll make a Scotswoman of her yet!' Bruce ruffled Jenny's pale gold hair with a friendly hand. He was wearing jeans and an open-necked shirt and looked younger and more carefree than Fiona had ever seen him. She glanced at Judi, who was sitting beside him.

Didn't it ever occur to her that Bruce really was rather an attractive person? Obviously, of course, he'd put her back up—tact wasn't Bruce's strong point and Judi certainly wasn't used to criticism of her behaviour!— but it was strange that she firmly refused to recognise any at all of his undoubted good points!

Rowan swept the launch round in a wide curve and they sped away down the loch. The four passengers watched the rocky shores slip past and did not speak, so that only the cries of the moorland birds disturbed the silence. The wind blew freshly in their faces and whipped Jenny's and Fiona's long hair this way and that.

'I should have brought a scarf,' thought Fiona as a strand of hers blew across Rowan's lean brown cheek and he put up a hand to brush it away.

'When Jenny finally consents to have her hair cut I'll probably have mine cut at the same time. It's a fearful nuisance on windy days, but I don't like to wear it up, except for formal occasions,' she said lightly.

'Oh, don't have it cut! You've always had long hair, ever since I can remember. Pigtails at eleven, a ponytail at fourteen.' Rowan turned his head and looked at her, a lurking smile in his eyes.

'I thought, Rowan, that you were supposed to have a bad memory?' Judi's voice sounded determinedly bright, but Fiona, detecting a slight hint of jealousy, answered her quickly.

'He has. I don't believe I ever had pigtails at eleven. I hated them!'

'Oh, but you did! I used to pull them,' Rowan said solemnly.

'How unkind! I wouldn't like anyone to do that to me!' Jenny said reproachfully. 'Did he ever make you cry, Mummy?'

'Never!' Rowan assured her. 'You were a tough little cookie, weren't you, Fiona? I never even made you cry the day I inadvertently blacked your eye with a cricket ball!'

No, thought Fiona bitterly, you didn't make me cry that day. Or ever, during our childhood. You had to wait until I was nearly grown-up. You made me cry then, all right—you'll never know how much I cried . . . .

Tight-lipped she said, 'Bruce and Judi will be bored stiff if we spend the whole day indulging in reminiscences of our childhood, Rowan. Can't we talk of something else?'

'Oh, but I like hearing about when you were a little girl!' Jenny exclaimed, and Rowan said smoothly, 'Another time, Jenny. Look at those stags over there! Aren't they splendid?'

It was a tactful diversion. There on the mountain slopes and close to the water stood three stags, two of them full-grown, with magnificent heads, and the third a youngster. He lacked the spread that his elders carried and his coat was a dingy brown compared with their brilliant russet.

By the time Jenny's delighted 'Ooohs!' and 'Aaaahs!' had been exhausted the launch was puffing away towards the upper loch, the hills falling apart and quiet green stretches of shining water appearing. Here it was very beautiful, very wild and very lonely, and to Jenny it seemed that the loch was going on for ever. Point after point, she declared with conviction, *must* be the end, but always it fell back at their approach to show yet another sleeping stretch beyond. Each reach narrowed, with the mountains growing always closer and steeper and their slopes more desolate and deserted.

93

'This really *is* the last point, Jenny,' Rowan said with a smile. 'Round the hill—wait just one minute—now, you see!'

The head of the loch was a quiet pool, the shimmering waters of which mirrored the sombre heights surrounding it. Jenny gazed around her wide-eyed.

'It's beautiful! Is this where we're going to have our picnic?'

'Hungry already?' Judi teased. She had, Fiona thought, been unusually quiet, but at least her grin had its usual spice of mischief.

'Starving,' Jenny said simply, and Fiona laughed and said, 'It's the mountain air. Smell it. Isn't it sweet?'

At Jenny's insistence a search was made for a picnic spot and they all settled down to enjoy the contents of the big wicker hamper. Rowan, a glint in his dark blue eyes, produced two gold-necked bottles and Judi, after one incredulous stare, gave a rapturous sigh.

'Champagne! Rowan darling!'

'I've had it on ice, so I hope it will be all right. I remembered that you once told me that it was—er—your favourite tipple.'

'It would be,' Bruce said a little sardonically, and Judi turned on him in a flash.

'What do you mean by that? Everyone likes champagne!' Then, as Bruce raised his brows, 'Oh no, I suppose *you* don't! You wouldn't admit to such decadent tastes!'

'Hey, I never said anything about not liking it!' Bruce protested, and Rowan, pouring champagne, shot him an amused look.

'Never try to justify yourself to a woman, my dear Bruce. It's a futile pursuit!—Shut up, Judi, and drink this,' and he handed first her, and then Fiona and Bruce, a glass of sunlit bubbles.

'Am I going to have some champagne, too?' Jenny asked with interest, and Rowan laughed.

'I doubt if you'd like it, Jenny. I brought some Coke for you!'

Bruce's contribution to the feast was a huge box of chocolates. Fiona, lazy and replete, stretched out on the soft bracken to watch the play of the sunlight on the surrounding hills. It was very quiet save for the sound of water, the calling of seagulls and the occasional bleating of sheep.

'I wish sheep didn't make such an unattractive sound. It's rather like a horrid sneering laugh,' she observed to no one in particular.

'They aren't very attractive animals, though I don't suppose I'd get Bruce to agree with me!' Judi, perhaps because of the influence of the champagne, was in a far better humour. 'No, for heaven's sake don't wave any more food in front of me, Jenny! I shan't be capable of moving a step as it is!'

Jenny's face fell. 'Oh! Aren't we going to explore? I thought perhaps we could climb that hill. There's a path—look!' and she pointed to a rough, stony track winding upwards.

Bruce and Judi groaned in unison and Rowan said unsympathetically, 'Serve you both right! If you will insist on making gluttons of yourselves—'

Judi, incensed, sat up and hurled a pebble at him. 'Rowan Macrae! Who was a bigger glutton than you?'

'Ah, but you can see that I'm not suffering from any ill effects,' Rowan said blandly. 'I'll climb the hill with you, Jenny.' Then, dropping his bantering tone, 'You'd be well advised to stay put anyway, Judi. I know that ankle of yours is nearly better, but there's

95

no point in taking unnecessary risks. You don't want to be laid up for another week.'

'Dear Rowan, I'm sure you're right!' Judi gave a little sigh of satisfaction and closed her eyes. 'We'll stay here and sleep, shall we, Fiona, and let those who wish to do so indulge in violent exercise!'

'Oh, but I want Mommy to come with Uncle Rowan and me,' Jenny protested, and caught hold of Fiona's hand. 'You will, won't you, Mommy?'

'Oh, darling! We can't leave poor Judi alone—' Fiona began, but Bruce interrupted her.

'No problem. I'll keep Judi company.'

A moment's silence. Judi's eyes had flown open. She looked from Bruce to Rowan, then said slowly, 'Well, okay. But don't be too long, you three, will you? Once the sun goes down it begins to get chilly.'

'I hope those two won't have come to blows by the time we get back!' Fiona, setting off along the stony path, could not resist a backward glance. Judi had resumed a recumbent position and Bruce was sitting hugging his knees, his eyes fixed on the far distant hills.

'They do rather seem to strike sparks off one another,' Rowan agreed. 'Pity. Buchanan's a good bloke, though he certainly knows more about handling a large estate than he does about handling women. Don't you find him a little lacking in—er—finesse, Fiona?'

Fiona shot him an angry look. 'The art of seduction may be something that he's not particularly anxious to excel in!' she said bitingly, and then wished she had held her tongue, for Rowan's eyes danced.

'That sounds remarkably like a put-down, Fiona. Come to think of it, you never lose an opportunity to insinuate that I'm something of a Casanova . . . a

96

breaker of female hearts. Why, for heaven's sake? Even allowing for local gossip your attitude seems a little exaggerated, to say the least of it!'

He paused, then as she did not answer added, 'I treated *you* very honourably, as I remember, far more honourably than you eventually treated me. Of course, I was young and chivalrous in those days and you, my sweet Fiona, were my particular bright star!'

Fiona's cheeks flamed at his light, mocking voice. Mercifully Jenny, as agile as a mountain sheep, had leapt ahead and so could not possibly have heard Rowan's remarks.

'Rowan, will you please stop——'

'Harking back to the past!' Rowan finished the sentence for her, his face suddenly grim. 'With each repetition your concern to draw a discreet veil over past events becomes more tedious, Fiona. You should let me have things out with you once and for all and then perhaps I'd stop teasing you!'

Jenny, far ahead, had stopped and was waiting with obvious impatience for them to catch up with her. Fiona, her lips compressed, her eyes stormy, began to hurry, ignoring Rowan and brushing past bracken and gorse bushes without a thought for scratched arms or torn slacks. She took good care, once she had reached Jenny's side, not to let the child get too far ahead again, though in any case the climb became so steep that she had no breath at all to spare for sparring.

They came at last to the broad bare summit of the hill. Jenny and Fiona, panting and breathless, dropped on to a flat rock and rested for a few moments while Rowan stood with his hands in his pockets and gazed about him. On each side they were surrounded by hills of many different shapes and colours and outlines and beyond them were the mountain peaks, faint and

W L—D

blue in the distance. Beneath them lay the wide shining loch, the glinting stars of sunlight catching its gentle ripples.

After a minute or two Jenny sprang up and went to join Rowan. Fiona, watching, saw the latter put a casual arm round the child's shoulders as he pointed out the various peaks and told her their names, and sudden tears blurred her eyes. She remembered what Rowan had said in the Edinburgh restaurant—that if things had not gone wrong between them Jenny might well have been his daughter.

Jenny was laughing at something Rowan had said, her pale little face rosy with her recent exertions, her grey eyes shining. She looked very small and frail beside Rowan, whose tall, muscular body, leaning slightly forward against the wind, suggested an easy strength. Looking at him as he smiled down at Jenny, Fiona wondered a little uneasily what he had meant when he had said, ' You should let me have things out with you once and for all. . . . '

Of course, although he couldn't have been really in love with her he must have hurt his pride badly when she'd sent him that cold little note telling him that she had changed her mind and that she was going to marry Neil and go to America with him. He hadn't known . . . had no way of knowing . . . that she had seen him with Tessa MacGregor, had heard the frightened girl's frenzied appeal and his own harsh rejection of it.

' For God's sake, Tessa, you don't know what you're saying! I can't help you—you know I can't. . . . '

She hadn't waited to hear any more. Her hands clapped over her ears, bewildered, stunned, and heart-broken she had fled from the scene. Tessa . . . in trouble! And Rowan responsible! Why else would she have turned to him?

It would have been a hideous shock even if she and Rowan had not been secretly engaged. 'The shortest engagement on record!' Fiona thought bitterly, remembering with a pang how she had insisted that for a little while nobody should be allowed to share their precious secret.

'I know exactly what will happen. We'll be deluged with congratulations and good wishes and everyone will start making plans for us and giving us good advice, and I don't think I could bear it, at least not yet! Please give me just a little time to get used to the miracle of your loving me!' she had begged, and Rowan had laughed and kissed her tenderly.

'Funny wee Fiona! But I know what you mean, darling, even though personally I'm longing to boast to everyone that I'm the luckiest chap in the world! I'd like to shout it from the hilltops for the whole world to hear. But we'll wait, if that's what you really want. Just for a few weeks, at any rate.'

Then, laughingly, he had added, 'Mind you, I don't think that either of us has a hope of being able to keep our secret if we meet in public! One look, and I should think that even the most unobservant of persons must guess that we're fathoms deep in love!'

Fiona had been deeply touched by his understanding, his complete willingness to put her wishes before his own. For just one week she had been so deliriously happy that sometimes she had wondered if even the angels in heaven did not envy her. It had never occurred to her, as with a singing heart she had slipped off to keep a secret tryst with her lover, that there might have been other, even more secret meetings for Rowan, that Tessa's vivid beauty had ensnared his senses if not his heart.

Tessa must have loved Rowan very deeply, she

99

thought sadly, her eyes still on the man's tall figure. She had certainly been loyal. It must have been entirely for his sake that she had never revealed to anyone that he was the father of her child. She would have realised, of course, the disastrous effect it might have had upon his career, just as she would also have realised that as a wife she could only be a handicap to the man she loved. Poor, poor Tessa. . . .

'Mommy!' Jenny was beckoning imperiously and slowly Fiona got to her feet and joined them. Rowan looked at her keenly.

'Feeling fagged, Fiona? You look rather pale.'

'I'm all right, thanks, but it was certainly quite a stiff climb.'

'Well worth it, I think, though,' Rowan observed.

Fiona drew a long breath. 'Oh yes, it's a marvellous view! Isn't it, Jenny?'

The child nodded vigorously. 'I know the names of all those mountains! Uncle Rowan's told me.'

Rowan glanced at his watch. 'I'm rather afraid we ought not to stay any longer. It's later than I thought.'

'I don't mind. I've had quite a nice little rest,' Jenny said cheerfully, and prepared to begin the downward descent.

Fiona checked her sharply. 'It's much harder going down than up, Jenny. You must let Rowan go in front, and follow him. I'll be right behind you.'

She turned to glance at Rowan for confirmation that he was ready to start and her foot slipped on a loose stone. She staggered, and might have fallen if Rowan's arm had not shot out. For a moment she was held hard against his body and she heard his sudden intake of breath, then, almost abruptly, he let her go.

'Seems to me that it's you who needs to be careful and not Jenny!' he said almost derisively, and Fiona, momentarily shaken off balance, furious that she had been affected by his nearness, snapped back, 'When I want your advice I'll ask for it!'

It was rather a silent little procession that later rejoined Judi and Bruce on the shores of the loch. Jenny never once complained, but it was obvious that she was very tired. Fiona, conscious of her own aching muscles, thought remorsefully that perhaps after all they ought not to have climbed so far and possibly Rowan shared her view. At any rate, though she firmly refused to be carried he helped Jenny all he could and his cheerful banter did much to keep up her spirits.

Fiona noted with a certain amount of relief that neither Judi nor Bruce bore the marks of any particularly spirited warfare. In fact they seemed to be on quite a friendly footing and there was genuine surprise in Judi's voice when, looking at her watch, she exclaimed, 'Goodness! Have you three really been gone nearly a couple of hours?'

'I'm glad you haven't missed us too much,' Rowan said, looking amused.

'We wouldn't dream of telling you if we had!' Judi retorted. 'You're quite conceited enough as it is, Rowan Macrae!'

Rowan held out his hand to help pull her to her feet. 'Don't you believe it! Fiona can always be relied upon to do a very good job of cutting me down to size!' he said placidly.

Fiona, busying herself with shaking leaves and pieces of bracken from the rugs that had been spread upon the ground, pretended not to hear. She was feeling vaguely depressed and put it down to the fact that, like Jenny, she was somewhat overtired. But not just physically in her case. Whenever she was thrown into

Rowan's company she could always feel her nerves tightening until they were as taut as bowstrings, and she also bitterly resented the discovery she had made that whether she liked it or not she was still susceptible to him physically. She knew with unhappy certainty that she would not find it easy to forget how her blood had tingled when, for those few brief seconds on the top of the hill, he had held her hard against him.

As Judi had predicted, it was becoming chilly and they were all glad of some coffee. Afterwards the vacuum flasks were stored with the picnic hamper in the stern of the launch and preparations were made for the journey back to Inveray.

At the stone landing slip Rowan smiled at Judi as Bruce helped her out of the launch. 'See you in about an hour,' he said cheerfully, and Fiona remembered that something had been said earlier about his taking Judi out to dinner. Well, she hadn't had him to herself all day. She would enjoy the chance of holding his undivided attention!

Bruce drove Fiona, Judi and Jenny back to Cragside and the first thing that Fiona did was to run Jenny's bath.

'I'll make the water a bit hotter than usual tonight, I think,' she told her daughter. 'It will take the ache out of your muscles!'

'My legs do ache, rather,' Jenny admitted grudgingly. 'But it was a lovely picnic, wasn't it, Mommy? I do think it was kind of Uncle Rowan to take us.'

'Yes, it was.' Fiona, testing the bath water with her elbow, did not look up.

'He's a lovely man,' Jenny said dreamily. 'The nicest man I've ever known. I wish—' She stopped abruptly.

Fiona straightened and stared at her. 'You wish

what?'

Jenny's face went pink. 'It doesn't matter.'

Fiona, who had a shrewd suspicion as to what had been in her daughter's mind, wisely refrained from pursuing the subject. A little while later, however, Jenny asked in a carefully casual voice, 'Is Judi going to marry Uncle Rowan, Mommy? I heard Granny telling someone that it was quite on the cards. What did she mean by that? I didn't understand.'

Mrs Campbell had obviously forgotten, just for one brief unguarded moment, that little pitchers had ears! Fiona thought grimly.

Aloud she said firmly, 'Little girls who listen in to adults' conversation will often hear things they don't understand, Jenny. When that happens it usually means that in no circumstances should they be repeated!'

'Yes, but—'

'Jenny, your bath is ready,' Fiona said austerely.

Jenny looked mutinous. 'But you haven't answered my question!'

'Because I can't,' Fiona told her crisply. 'I don't know any more about it than you do.'

'Oh!' Jenny digested that. Then she stepped into the bath and said pensively, more to herself than to her mother, 'I think Uncle Rowan is a *lot* nicer than Uncle Steve!'

In spite of herself Fiona had to choke back a rueful laugh. Jenny had never been particularly keen on Steve and that was yet another reason why she, Fiona, had consistently refused to marry him. Steve was quite fond of Jenny, in a mild sort of way, but he didn't understand children and was also a little impatient of Fiona's devotion to her daughter. He didn't like feeling that he was an 'also ran', though in a sense, of course, that was just what he was.

Fiona left Jenny soaking luxuriously in a hot bath and went downstairs to prepare her a supper tray. She could hear Judi carolling blissfully in the second bathroom and smiled a little bleakly. Judging from the spectacular dress she had just noticed spread out on Judi's bed, the younger girl was out to make a big impression tonight. Well, good luck to her.

Mrs Campbell was on the telephone and was still deep in conversation when a few minutes later Fiona heard the sound of Rowan's car in the driveway. The doorbell rang, and she realised with annoyance that she would have to be the one to answer it.

She had forgotten, until she saw Rowan's brows lift in faint amusement, that she was still wearing the voluminous apron that from force of habit she had donned when bathing Jenny. It was of crisp blue gingham and though she did not know it, it suited her admirably. Certainly there was a glint of something that might have been appreciation in Rowan's dark blue eyes, though Fiona chose to ignore it.

' I don't suppose Judi will be very long. Won't you go and sit in the drawing room? I believe Uncle is in there watching a television programme,' she said.

' Then I won't interrupt him. He'd turn the set off immediately and it may be something in which he's really interested,' Rowan said, and followed Fiona into the kitchen. He perched himself on the edge of the table, svelte and handsome in a faultlessly cut dinner jacket and a silk shirt, and watched her as she poured milk into a glass. She hoped he wouldn't notice that her hands were trembling.

' You really are at pains to avoid my company, aren't you, Fiona? I think you must have a guilty conscience or something, though I assure you that it's quite unnecessary.'

Rowan's eyes were bright with derisive amusement as he added, ' Just because I'm human enough to be curious about your past behaviour it doesn't necessarily mean that I'm in any way inclined to blame you for it. Neil was a far better catch than I was, and you were a sensible girl to realise it before it was much too late.'

Fiona flared at the ironic bite of his words. ' That's an abominable thing to say!'

' Is it, Fiona?' He looked at her, his mouth hard, his eyes dark and compelling. ' Then if you didn't ditch me for materialistic reasons the truth must be that you were never really in love with me at all. That you were just messing me around, as the saying goes. Is that why you were so painfully anxious to keep our engagement a secret, because you were in love with Neil all the time?'

' Rowan, please——' She tried to brush past him, but his hands shot out and grabbed her wrists.

' Oh, no, Fiona! This time you're going to tell me what I want to know. Answer my question, please.'

She tried to wrench herself free. ' Rowan, you're hurting me!'

' Then keep still!' he retorted savagely.

She bit her lip. The temptation to tell him that she knew all about Tessa was almost too strong for her, but she resisted it fiercely. In the first place she had no right to the knowledge she possessed and, in the second, if she blurted it out now there was a very real danger that someone might overhear. Judi, for instance. . . .

Her pulses thudding, she said breathlessly, ' You *know* why I changed my mind! Why do we have to go back over it? I——I can't stand it! It's all over and

105

forgotten, or if it isn't it ought to be! You can't resurrect something that happened over eight years ago!'

She stopped and swallowed. 'I behaved badly, perhaps, but I was young and—and terribly emotional and unbalanced, especially as I'd just lost Father. You—you rather knocked me sideways by telling me that you loved me. I—I suppose I was flattered and—and anyway I *was* fond of you, I really was.'

She stopped again, biting her lip as Rowan said slowly, 'But you were even fonder of Neil? Is that what you're going to tell me?'

'I . . . yes. Yes, that's it. Please, Rowan, can't we just *leave* it there? I—I can't. . . .'

Rowan's face was inscrutable as he dropped her wrists. She stood staring at the marks made by his fingers as he said very gently, 'All right, Fiona. I still think you're keeping something back, but if you don't want to tell me I suppose there's nothing I can do to make you.'

Fiona knew that tears were perilously near the surface. In a voice which shook a little despite her efforts to control it she said, 'I can't think why you're at all interested. We don't mean anything to each other now. Surely the time for all this was eight years ago? You accepted my decision to marry Neil without a word of protest. You never even answered my letter. . . .'

Rowan gave her a twisted little smile. 'Oh, did that rankle? Poor Fiona! I'm sorry if I disappointed you by refusing to act the part of the jealous, frantic lover.' He paused, then added a little bitterly, 'If you really want to know I think my main reason for keeping quiet was hurt pride. It's something to reckon with, you know, at the age of twenty-two.'

Yes, she thought bleakly, that was it . . . hurt pride.

He had never forgiven or forgotten the blow she had dealt to his ego. He hadn't really loved her, but nonetheless her defection had rankled. Obviously it still did, even now. . . .

' Hello there! I'm ready!' a gay voice said behind them, and Judi appeared in the doorway. She was wearing a close-fitting amber dress, with her dark hair drawn back from her face to show the delicate contours of her cheeks and her lips painted a soft rosy red. She looked gay and beautiful, and Rowan's, ' Mmmm! My million dollar girl!' brought an additional sparkle to her dark eyes.

' 'Bye, Fiona.' Rowan's farewell could not have been more careless. It was as though now that he had found out what he had wanted to know he had lost interest in her completely.

' Goodbye. . . .' She watched them go, a lump in her throat. What she wanted to do, she told herself miserably, was cry and cry . . . and she couldn't. Jenny would certainly want to know the reason for any tear-stains. And in any case she had already wept all the tears that she was going to weep over Rowan Macrae, eight years ago. She certainly wasn't going to start all over again, not when it would be just as stupid, just as futile.

CHAPTER VII

The red and gold pageantry of October gave way to the soft grey mistiness of November.

Several times Fiona reluctantly decided that she must broach the subject of her return to America, but each time her courage failed her. She could not help but realise what a difference she and Jenny had made to the lonely lives of the Campbells and how sorry her in-laws would be to see them go. Judi, it was true, was still at Cragside, but to everyone's surprise she had found herself a job working as a part-time typist for Inveray's one celebrity, an elderly author whose detective novels usually sold many thousands of copies.

'What luck I taught myself to type, ages and ages ago!' she said cheerfully to Fiona. 'I like Mr Paterson, he's an old darling, and his book's frightfully exciting, I'm simply longing for him to reach the final chapter so I know who dun it! At the moment I *think* it's either the voluptuous film-star or else her batty secretary, but Mr Paterson just grins when I ask him if I'm right! It really is frustrating! I mean, if one buys a detective story one can always turn straightaway to the back, at least that's what *I* do, and I'm sure that there must be hundreds of other people who do exactly the same thing!'

Fiona looked at her in amusement. 'Have you abandoned all your acting ambitions, then?'

'Well, I told you that I never was a really good actress,' Judi said candidly. 'I'm not a very good typist, either, come to that, but Mr Paterson doesn't seem to mind too much. It's only a temporary job, you know: he's got a secretary only she's away nursing a sick sister or something.'

She stretched her slim brown arms above her head and added, with her gamin grin, 'Actually this job serves a two-fold purpose. It provides me with a reasonable excuse to stay at Inveray so that I'm still within Rowan's orbit, and it also proves to Bruce that I'm not really such a lazy layabout after all!'

'I don't believe he's ever thought that of you, Judi.'

'Oh, he has! But I'm beginning to understand Bruce a bit better now, Fiona. That day we had the picnic and you and Rowan and Jenny went off by yourselves we had quite an interesting talk. He told me that his father died when he was only nine, leaving absolutely no money and a pile of debts, and his mother worked like a *slave* to pay off all the creditors and give Bruce and his two brothers a reasonable upbringing as well. She died when Bruce was twenty.'

She paused, then added pensively, 'I think he somehow feels a constant need to justify all the sacrifices that his mother made for him. Or perhaps by working as hard as he does he feels he's making up for some of his father's shortcomings. He didn't actually say so, you know, but I rather gathered that Buchanan père really *was* a lazy good-for-nothing if there ever was one! Funny to think of Bruce with a father like that, isn't it? I suppose he takes after his mother.'

Fiona was staring at her in surprise, for Judi was rarely serious, let alone analytical. Judi met her startled gaze and grinned again.

'*I* think Bruce needs reforming much more than I do! I'm doing my level best to make him realise that life really isn't half as grim as he thinks it is, and that having a bit of fun now and again isn't a violation of any unwritten commandment! I'm succeeding, I really am. He's becoming quite recognisably a human being!'

'Judi, you're impossible!' Fiona said, laughing. Privately she thought that the quiet, rather solemn Bruce made an excellent foil for the mercurial Judi, but she could not help hoping that he would not take her attempts to 'humanise' him too seriously. It was still Rowan who was Judi's *beau ideal*, even though he seemed remarkably slow to take advantage of the fact.

He had been an infrequent visitor at Cragside since the day of the picnic, ostensibly because of an outbreak of influenza in the district which had laid a good proportion of the population low. Unfortunately the victims had also included old Dr Macrae, which meant that Fiona's and Jenny's visit to him had had to be indefinitely postponed. Although she was sorry for the reason, Fiona was a little relieved that for the time being, at least, she was not to be thrown into any close proximity with Rowan. She was still very unsure of him and of his attitude towards her, and in addition her own feelings were hopelessly troubled and confused. Why, when she knew that the way that Rowan had behaved was utterly indefensible, was she herself nagged by such a sense of guilt? It wasn't sensible . . . but then there had never been anything sensible about her relationship with Rowan. It had, quite simply, been the one and only thing that had ever really mattered. . . .

It was a further complication to begin receiving from Steve Connaught, back in America, urgent letters imploring her to return as soon as possible.

'You have already been away far too long,' he wrote in one. 'The longer you delay your return, Fiona, the harder you will find it. I realise how sympathetic you must be feeling towards Neil's parents, but you have told me so many times that your future lies in this country that I refuse to believe that in just a few weeks you have begun to change your mind. . . .'

Fiona sighed as she laid the letter down and looked across to where her father-in-law was sitting by the window, reading a newspaper. He could still see to read a little, but only with great difficulty and by using a very strong magnifying glass. He was due to see an American specialist when the great man came to London at the end of the month, but nobody dared to build too many hopes on the outcome of the consultation. It was merely a last chance and only a very slight one at that.

Perhaps Douglas Campbell felt the intensity of Fiona's troubled gaze, for he lifted his head and smiled at her.

'You look worried, Fiona. Is there anything wrong, my dear? Not bad news in your letter, I hope.'

Fiona shook her head. 'No. Not bad news. It's from a friend in America.'

Mr Campbell smiled a little sadly. 'Asking when you propose to return, no doubt! I don't forget, my dear, that originally you came for only a short visit. It's more than good of you to prolong your stay when I'm sure you would really prefer to return to the life you've made for yourself in America and the friends who have helped you,' he said gently.

Fiona coloured. Had Jenny been talking about 'Uncle Steve' to her grandparents? she wondered uneasily.

As if Douglas Campbell read her thoughts he stretched out his hand to her. 'My dear, much as we love having you and Jenny with us we would never willingly stand in the way of your happiness. You are still a very young and beautiful woman and it would only be natural if you were thinking of marrying again. You owe nothing, now, to Neil's memory. He would want you to have a second chance, just as we do,' he said gently.

Fiona's eyes blurred with sudden tears. 'You're both so kind to me—'

'We are proud to have you as a daughter.' Douglas Campbell hesitated, then added, 'I think perhaps you ought to know that originally Margaret and I had a few misgivings over Neil's marriage. We were very much afraid that it had been too hasty and ill-considered and that either one—or both of you—might have cause to regret it. It wasn't that we had cause to doubt the sincerity of your affection for each other, but the circumstances were so very odd and you yourself, Fiona, were so unnaturally bright and gay . . .' He broke off and shook his head.

'I don't know why I'm harking back to all that! What I'm really trying to say is that Margaret and I are both sure that for the brief time your marriage lasted you made Neil very, very happy, and for that we are both deeply grateful.'

Fiona had gone very pale. It wasn't true, she thought miserably. She hadn't managed to make Neil happy—quite the reverse, though it hadn't been altogether her fault. Neil had guessed that an aching sense of loss had lived on in her heart and it had aroused him to a frenzy of jealousy. He had, at times, behaved with complete unreasonableness.

She shivered inwardly at the memory of his harsh treatment, then resolutely put it from her. She could serve no useful purpose by telling the Campbells the truth about her marriage. It was kinder to let them think that it had, in fact, been a completely happy union. It was far too late to regret the impulse that had made her accept Neil's impassioned proposals . . . too late to regret that because of her youth and inexperience she had failed to foresee the complications that might occur. Now Neil was dead, and the sense of guilt that still nagged at her was her constant punishment for having married a man she did not love.

Mr Campbell was still speaking. 'I'd like to ask you a favour, Fiona. Upstairs there are some letters, diaries and photographs which belonged to Neil and which Margaret and I have long felt ought to be disposed of, though neither of us has felt equal to the task. Would you, my dear, be kind enough to sort through the things for us, keeping anything that you feel might be of interest to Jenny and disposing of the rest?'

Fiona nodded. 'Yes, I'll do that.' It was the least she could do for her in-laws, she thought, though she knew already that it was not a task which she would find easy.

Neil's old room had not been slept in since he left Cragside and to Fiona it shrieked of emptiness, a mere shell that had once housed a vivid personality. The papers Douglas Campbell had referred to were in a box on a chair and Fiona sat down on the chintz-covered divan bed to sort through them. She quickly realised that nearly everything related to Neil's schooldays: the photographs were mostly of school groups and cricket teams and a slim, black leather diary bore scrawled entries for the year that Neil had been fourteen. She laid that aside for closer inspection later, and turned her attention to the photographs. Neil, she knew, had never been in any of his school teams, but Rowan had captained both the rugger and cricket sides besides being a useful footballer and a better-than-average tennis player.

There was something odd about the photographs.

113

Fiona frowned down at them and then saw what it was. In three of them a face had been obliterated by being scratched out with a penknife. But *whose* face? And why?

The answer to her first question dawned on her slowly. It must be Rowan's, since otherwise he was missing from the photographs. But why? Why should Neil have behaved so childishly, especially as Rowan was supposed to be his best friend?

It was the diary that gave her the clue. Most of the entries were brief and uninteresting, but one was almost startlingly explicit.

' Rowan has won the Drummond essay prize for the second year running, though this time I did think that I stood a good chance,' the boy Neil had written in large, unformed handwriting. ' It isn't fair, I'm sure my essay was better than his, but when I said something about favouritism all the other chaps ragged me and said I was jealous. Rowan told me afterwards that he hadn't realised I wanted the prize so badly, but that was a lie, of course he knew. Just wait. One day I'm going all out to get something that Rowan wants and then perhaps we'll see how he likes having to play second fiddle. . . .'

Fiona put the diary down feeling bewildered . . . almost shocked. Of course Neil had been very young when he wrote that particular entry, but was there any reason why his attitude should have changed as he grew older? Success in work and games had come so easily to Rowan and he had been so popular with everyone. Certainly Neil, less able in almost every direction, had never indicated to anyone that he was jealous of his friend, but it looked from this diary as though the seeds of resentment might have been sown very early on.

She stared at the photographs again, her expression uneasy. There was something here she did not quite understand. Something dark and ugly that was better left hidden.

With sudden resolution she ripped the photographs in half, then tore the pages out of the diary. There was no point in keeping them. She made a bundle of all the unwanted papers and was about to add a tattered copy of Wisden—dated the year of her marriage to Neil and consequently hopelessly out of date—when a slip of paper fluttered out of it and on to the floor. Retrieving it, she saw that it was a piece of paper torn out of a notebook and that it bore a few words in a straggling, somewhat unformed hand.

' Sorry I couldn't make it last night. Dad wanted me to help him with something and I couldn't manage to get away. I'll wait at the usual place tomorrow without fail. Have something very important to tell you. Please be there, Neil darling.'

Fiona's brows drew together in a bewildered frown. Who on earth could have sent Neil a message like that? Obviously it was from a girl, but Neil, to the best of her knowledge, had never had any girl-friends before he married her. Not like Rowan, who'd made no secret of the fact that he'd dated any number.

' Have something very important to tell you. Please be there, Neil darling. . . .' Fiona eyed the words uneasily, but at last she shrugged and tore the paper in half, like the photographs. She would never know the identity of the writer, or what the ' something important ' had been. Quite likely it hadn't been anything important at all, really.

She picked up the bundle and took it downstairs to the dustbin. She couldn't help thinking, as she did so, how odd it was that even though Neil had been her husband she had never known him half as well as she had known Rowan. Neil had had hidden depths. During those first few months in America she had felt sometimes as though she had married a complete stranger.

When she had completed her task she returned to the library to report to her father-in-law, but found him talking to Bruce, who rose to his feet as she entered the room.

'Hello, Fiona.' Then, as she hesitated, 'Don't think you're interrupting anything. We've just finished our discussion and I'm off home now.'

'Home', for Bruce, was a little cottage on the estate. Fiona had never been inside, but she had learned from Judi that it was kept spotlessly clean and that Bruce was absolutely self-sufficient.

Now she smiled at him. 'I wanted to see you so that I could thank you for giving my daughter another riding lesson yesterday. She thoroughly enjoyed it. As a reward——at least let's hope it's that!——I've baked you a cake. Somebody said you were rather susceptible to chocolate sponges: I hope it's true!'

Douglas Campbell gave her a sharp look which, perhaps luckily, she did not notice. 'You're in luck, Bruce. Fiona is an excellent cook.'

'I'm sure she is. It was a nice thought, Fiona, and I'm sure I shall enjoy the cake, whatever effect it has upon my waistline!' Bruce said, laughing. 'Can I collect it now?'

'Of course. I'll get it for you.'

They crossed the hall together and as they did so Judi emerged from the study, looking thoroughly disgruntled.

'Hello. Why the scowl?' Bruce asked lightly.

'Because I'd got a date with Rowan tonight, the first

for simply ages, and he's just rung up to say he can't make it! Someone's very ill with pneumonia, so of course he says he **can't** leave him,' Judi said gloomily.

'You wouldn't have him leave his patient just to keep a date with you, would you?' Bruce asked gently.

'Of course I wouldn't! Don't be silly, Bruce! It's just that—oh, I don't know why people ever *become* doctors! It's an awful life!'

'Who is it who is so ill?' Fiona asked quietly. 'Did Rowan tell you?'

Judi shrugged. 'Yes, but the name didn't convey a thing to me. Duncan MacGregor! Do you know him, Fiona? I don't.'

Duncan MacGregor! Tessa MacGregor's father— the man who had disowned her! Fiona caught her breath. Tessa was his only living relative. Now that he was seriously ill, would the girl be summoned to his bedside? More important still, would she come?

She realised that both Judi and Bruce were waiting for her to answer. She said slowly, 'Yes, I know him, but not at all well.'

She had a momentary vision of a big, burly man who had always seemed to epitomise rude good health. In fact, one of his proudest boasts had always been that he had never needed a doctor in his life.

'According to Rowan he had 'flu and neglected it. He tried to carry on just the same as usual and pneumonia is the result,' Judi explained. 'Rowan says that of course he ought to be in hospital, but at the moment he's much too ill to be moved.'

It was an ironic situation, Fiona thought—Rowan fighting for the life of a man whose daughter he had treated so shamefully. Not, of course, that he would ever think of it in those terms. To him, at the moment, Duncan MacGregor would merely be a very sick man who needed every bit of his skill and care.

Aloud she said quietly, ' I hope he'll be all right.'

' So do I.' Judi, making an obvious effort to shake off the gloom which had descended upon her, flicked back her dark hair. ' Oh well! I suppose an evening by the fire has something to recommend it, even if at the moment I can't work up much enthusiasm for liver and bacon! That's what we're having, aren't we, Fiona?'

Bruce pushed his ancient pipe down into a pocket of his corduroy jacket. ' I suppose you wouldn't accept me as a sort of substitute for Macrae, Judi? I could do with having dinner out myself: I believe I forgot to get anything for tonight,' he said amiably.

Fiona did not believe that for a single instant, but Judi, after an incredulous ' Are you *sure*? I mean, it would be heaven, but I really wasn't *fishing*!' accepted rapturously and rushed away to get ready.

Bruce's eyes met Fiona's and he grinned. ' I wasn't telling fibs, honestly, though I could tell by your expression that you thought I was. Mind you, I've got any number of tins that I could have opened, plus of course your chocolate cake, but—'

' But a four-course dinner will be that much more attractive!' Fiona said, laughing. ' I'm glad you thought of stepping into the breach, Bruce. I really don't think that Judi would have been at all happy with liver and bacon!'

Bruce glanced at her, hesitated, then said wryly, ' I thought she might be prepared to put up with me since there was no one else available. She thinks a lot of Macrae, doesn't she?'

' Yes, I'm afraid she does.'

' H'm. I rather think that quite a lot of it's just hero-worship left over from her childhood,' Bruce said with a flash of shrewdness, and after one surprised moment Fiona thought, ' He could be right at that. . . .'

Then she forgot all about Judi and Bruce and even Rowan in her concern for Duncan MacGregor. She learned later that evening that Tessa had been sent for directly Rowan had discovered the gravity of her father's illness, but that she had not yet arrived.

'I hope she won't be too late, poor girl. She used to think a lot of her father before—well, before all the trouble,' Mrs Campbell said. And then, ' To think that Duncan MacGregor has brought this on himself! He's always sworn he'd have nothing to do with doctors, but this time his stubbornness has cost him mighty dear. If Rowan had been able to treat him earlier—but there, where's the sense in talking like that?'

It was not until late the next day that Fiona learned that not only had Tessa MacGregor arrived at Inveray but that her father, though still seriously ill, had been pronounced out of danger. Her informant was the village postmistress. Between praising Rowan for his skill and devotion and denouncing Duncan Macgregor for his stupidity, the good lady also had much to say about Tessa.

' Aye, 'tis to be hoped that noo the puir lass is hame agin the breach 'twixt her and Duncan will be healed for gude and a',' she said, shaking her head. ' 'Tis a wumman's hand young Robbie needs, and Tessa's a gude lass, for a' she used to be sich a wild one in the auld- days. Let bygones be bygones, that's what I say. Dinna ye agree, Miss Fiona?'

Fiona, anxious to make her escape, said that she did. On her way home she caught a glimpse of Rowan as he drove past in his car. He held up his hand in a brief salute but did not stop. He looked tired and preoccupied, and Fiona wondered unhappily if this was not only because of the struggle he had had to put up to save Duncan MacGregor's life but because Tessa's return to Inveray was an unwanted complication in his life. While she had been safely tucked away in Glasgow, she thought bitterly, he had probably managed to forget all about her. Now, even if he had no conscience concerning her, it might not be quite so easy to ignore her existence.

It was a relief, when she got home, to find that Judi had arrived before her and was in a sparkling mood. No one could feel depressed for long in Judi's company: her effervescent personality could lift even the heaviest spirits.

'I'm sure I'm right, Fiona! It *is* the batty secretary!' she announced gaily as she seized a loaf and began to butter and cut thin slices. 'There's a blood-stain on her mackintosh!'

Her aunt, not surprisingly, stared at her in complete mystification. 'There's *what*?'

Judi laughed. 'It's all right, Auntie. Fiona knows what I'm talking about!' She had been slicing away rapidly and with skill, but now she paused and waved the bread-knife in mid-air. 'I think perhaps I'll try writing a detective novel myself. I'm sure I could think up quite an exciting plot!'

'I'm sure you could. The way you're brandishing that bread-knife is positively lethal!' Fiona removed herself to a safe distance as she spoke.

Judi giggled. 'Sorry. I get carried away sometimes. Like Bruce last night. D'you know, Fiona, we didn't get home until two o'clock? Isn't that shocking?'

'Scandalous!' Fiona agreed solemnly. 'I gather you enjoyed yourselves?'

'*I* did. I think Bruce did, too. He improves on acquaintance, that man.' She paused, then added casually, ' By the way, who is the red-haired beauty in our midst?'

' Red-haired beauty?'

' Mr Paterson happened to mention that he'd seen Rowan this morning and that he'd been talking to a frightfully attractive girl with lovely red-gold hair. She had a little boy with her, apparently.'

It was Mrs Campbell who answered. ' I expect that would be Tessa MacGregor, Duncan MacGregor's daughter.'

' Oh!' Judi knew nothing of Tessa's history, it seemed, for her expression was blank. ' How is he? Duncan MacGregor, I mean?'

' I think he's out of danger, but of course he'll need careful nursing. Directly he's well enough to be moved he's being transferred to hospital, I believe.' Mrs Campbell glanced towards Fiona. ' He was glad to see Tessa, I'm told, and she's promised to stay until he's better. It's my guess that he's been eating his heart out for her for a long time, though he was too proud and too stubborn to do anything about it.'

' Very likely.' Fiona answered briefly, unwilling to discuss Tessa lest by look or word she should inadvertently reveal that she knew more about her than anyone else. How strange it was, she thought, that after so many years first she, and then Tessa, had come back into Rowan's life! It couldn't possibly be a situation to his liking, but at least he had no need to fear that Tessa would break her long silence. Had she been tempted to reveal the name of the man with whom she had become so tragically involved she would have done so a long time ago.

Despite herself she felt a certain curiosity regarding

121

Tessa and it was a curiosity that was satisfied, purely by chance, only a few days later. She and Jenny were by the loch, watching the seagulls as they swooped low over the water, when a sturdy, red-haired boy wearing jeans and a polo-necked sweater approached them. Older than Jenny, he was also much bigger and strikingly handsome, with rosy cheeks and bright eyes.

'Hello. What's your name?' Jenny smiled at him without a trace of shyness.

'Robbie MacGregor. What's yours?'

'Jenny Campbell. Do you live here? I've just come on a visit.'

Robbie nodded. 'Yes, I know.'

Fiona had guessed almost from the first who the boy must be because of his distinctive red hair. She stared at him intently, realising that despite his colouring he did not really resemble his elder sister at all. His eyes were hazel, not green like Tessa's, and he looked as though he had a much more placid temperament.

A young woman had come out of a nearby cottage and was walking towards them. Fiona caught her breath as she half-recognised the slender, graceful figure and the creamy oval face. And, of course, the red-gold hair was unmistakable.

'Robbie, it's time for your milk—' the girl began, and then stopped and looked blankly at Fiona. 'Why, it's Fiona!' Then, flushing a little, 'Or should I say . . . Mrs Campbell?'

'Just Fiona will do.' Somehow Fiona managed to smile. Goodness, how Tessa had changed! It was almost unbelievable. Gone was the wild, rebellious-looking teenager she had known eight years ago and in her place was a mature and beautiful woman who looked rather older than her twenty-six years. She carried herself with a quiet dignity and when she spoke it was only the soft lilt to her voice that betrayed her Scottish origin.

There was a moment's silence. Then Fiona said, forcing herself to speak naturally, 'It's nice to see you again, Tessa. I was very sorry to hear about your father's illness: I hope he's going to be all right now?'

'I think so,' Tessa said quietly. 'Of course it'll be a while before he's completely fit again, but he's through the worst, thank goodness. He's in hospital now: I was told that he really ought to have round-the-clock attention for a few days, at least, and of course I couldn't give him that, not with Robbie to look after as well. He's away from school at the moment with ear trouble, but it isn't anything serious, thank goodness.'

Before Fiona could answer Jenny, who had been talking animatedly with Robbie, clutched her arm excitedly.

'Mommy, Mommy! Robbie's got a hamster! May I see it, please? Oh, please say I may!'

'Oh, darling, I hardly think—' Fiona began, but Tessa intervened quickly.

'It won't be any trouble, if that's what you're thinking.' She hesitated. 'I've—I've just made some coffee—'

It was impossible to refuse, Fiona thought. Anyway, why should she? She certainly felt no inclination to condemn Tessa on moral grounds: in fact, she felt nothing but sympathy towards her. The events of the past years had left their mark on her, for although she was more beautiful than ever there was a tautness on her face and a disquieting sadness in her eyes when she was not actually smiling.

The tiny cottage was in apple-pie order. While Robbie and Jenny occupied themselves with the hamster, Tessa poured out coffee for herself and Fiona and they exchanged news.

'I'm very happy in Glasgow,' Tessa said quietly, in answer to Fiona's hesitant question. 'I've a job that I enjoy and a very nice flat which I share with a couple of friends. The only thing that's worried me has been my father's attitude towards me. I suppose it's awful of me, but—but I can't bring myself to feel too sorry about his illness since it's brought us together again. I—I've missed him, these last few years.'

'I'm sure you have.'

Tessa twisted her spoon between her fingers. 'You must miss Mr Neil.' Her voice sounded stilted and unnatural as if, Fiona thought, she found it difficult to talk of someone who was dead. Her eyes went to Jenny, who was exclaiming over Robbie's hamster. 'You must be very glad that you've got a little girl.'

'Yes, I am.'

'You're going back to America pretty soon, aren't you? At least, that's what Rowan told me.'

Fiona stiffened in spite of herself. It seemed all wrong that Tessa should be able to refer to Rowan so casually. Did she feel no bitterness towards him? no resentment of any kind?

It was almost as if Tessa knew what she was thinking. At any rate she added quietly, 'He takes me to the hospital each day to see Father. It's more than good of him considering how busy he is, but he and his father have always been kind. I owe them a lot.'

Fiona put down her coffee cup and rose abruptly to her feet. Tessa's attitude towards Rowan, so different from her own, bewildered and almost angered her. Rowan had wrought havoc in her life and yet she could talk of his 'kindness'!

'I must go now, Tessa. Thank you for the coffee: it was lovely. I—I'll see you again, perhaps.'

124

She was about to call Jenny when there was a brisk tap on the door. Tessa called 'Come in' and, unexpectedly, it was Rowan who appeared. Neither Tessa nor Fiona had heard the car.

'Hello, Tessa! I've just popped in to have another look at Robbie's ears and to tell you—' He broke off as he saw Fiona and said, 'Hello! What are you doing here?'

There was something in his expression which was oddly inimical, and Fiona, feeling that she was being regarded as an intruder, flushed a little as she explained that Robbie had invited Jenny to see his hamster. 'We're just going,' she added hastily.

'Then in that case I'll give you a lift,' Rowan said coolly. 'I've only dropped by to give Tessa a message.'

Fiona opened her mouth to say that she preferred to walk and then closed it again. Far better to accept gracefully.

At that point Robbie came in from the garden, followed by Jenny. He stopped short when he saw Rowan and gave him a wide smile.

'Hello, Dr Macrae! Look at my hamster!'

'Hello, Robbie.' Rowan ruffled the curly red head as he bent to examine the hamster that Jenny held carefully in her hands. Fiona, glancing instinctively towards Tessa, surprised by such an expression of yearning sadness on the lovely face that inwardly she flinched. So Tessa did care, even now. . . . And Rowan? Was he perhaps beginning to regret the fact that he had lacked the courage to make Tessa his wife, eight years ago? If the lovely but untamed girl had stirred his senses didn't the beautiful, poised young woman she had become attract him even more?

She took a steadying breath. 'We'll wait for you

outside, Rowan.' She tried to laugh. 'You're so big, you take up nearly all the room!'

Rowan nodded. 'All right. I won't be a minute.'

The minute stretched to five and to Fiona, waiting impatiently for him to emerge, they felt like fifty. She was horrified to realise that the twisting pain in her heart was plain, simple jealousy. Why? She'd never felt jealous of Judi, however many times she had been out with Rowan!

She bit her lip. The answer to that was that Rowan's attitude to Judi wasn't in the least loverlike. He simply didn't seem to take her seriously. But Tessa . . . Tessa was different.

'Sorry to have kept you waiting.' Rowan shot Fiona a swift penetrating look as he finally emerged from the cottage, but she studiously ignored his gaze. Unfortunately for her peace of mind, however, her air of chilly detachment was only skin-deep. Rowan brushed her arm as he got into the car beside her and though it was the merest touch it left her shaken as by an earthquake.

Jenny, sitting in the back, was silent, not from choice but because Robbie, as a parting present, had given her an enormous mint humbug.

'You look as though you've got raging toothache!' Rowan teased her. 'I've never seen such bulging cheeks!' Then to Fiona, 'Nice to see Tessa back in Inveray, isn't it? What with you and her we seem to have nearly our full complement of prodigal daughters!'

Fiona could not trust herself to speak and after a moment Rowan gave a somewhat rueful little laugh.

'Sorry. That was an exceedingly stupid remark, especially as I didn't offer to give you a lift in order to quarrel with you! I wanted to talk to you about your father-in-law. You know he's seeing Professor Aiken, the famous American eye specialist, when he comes to attend a conference in Edinburgh next week?'

'Yes.' Fiona hesitated, swallowing her resentment. 'Don't they call him the miracle man?'

'He's certainly a brilliant surgeon, someone who combines an exceptional brain with inspired hands. I don't know about miracles, but I do know that if there's only the remotest chance of saving a patient's sight, he's prepared to take it. Anyway, I think it's just possible that in Mr Campbell's case he'll recommend an operation. If he does, it will be a risky business and nobody will know for several weeks whether the outcome is likely to be successful or not. It will be an anxious time for everyone concerned and I'm bound to say that I think your help and support could probably be invaluable.'

Fiona's hands clenched on her lap. 'Do you—do you mean that you don't think I ought to go back to the States just yet?'

Rowan was staring straight ahead of him. 'Would a few more weeks make so much difference to you? Or '—she saw his lips twist into a grim little smile— 'your good friend Steve Connaught?'

Fiona thought she detected a note of sarcasm in his smooth voice and her hackles rose instantly. Recklessly she said, 'I am missing Steve, yes, and I want to see him again very badly. But you haven't really left me much choice in the matter, have you?' She paused and swallowed. 'I—I'll stay until after Christmas.'

They drove on in silence for a few moments until Rowan slowed down to take a bend. Then he turned his head and smiled at her, the sudden attractive smile that had the power to make a traitor of her heart.

'Good,' he said, and Fiona thought confusedly, 'Why, he sounds as though he really means it!' And then, 'But of course he's only thinking of the welfare of his patient.'

CHAPTER VIII

Fiona waited until after Douglas Campbell had been examined by Professor Aiken before she wrote to Steve telling him of her decision to remain in Scotland for a few weeks longer.

'Professor Aiken says that if there is any chance at all of my father-in-law's sight being saved—or even partially saved—an immediate operation is imperative,' she wrote. 'It will be at least a month after that before we know whether he has, in fact, been able to work another miracle, so that I don't think that there is much chance of our being able to return to Miami before the New Year.'

Steve would be simply furious, she thought wryly as she sealed and stamped the letter. He had been an orphan since early childhood and so did not really understand the strength of family ties. He would not, she felt sure, appreciate her motives for prolonging her visit, nor would he feel the slightest sympathy with Douglas Campbell. In some ways he was a hard man . . . much harder than Rowan, for instance.

She frowned to herself, annoyed that she should ever have been tempted to compare the two men. At least one knew exactly where one stood with Steve, whereas Rowan, with that habit he had of shifting from satire to solicitude and back again within the space of just a few seconds, was completely baffling.

She slipped the letter into the pocket of her cardigan. No wonder poor Jùdi was beginning to feel the strain of a friendship which seemed to be leading exactly nowhere! Her gaiety occasionally seemed a little forced and there were times when all the vitality seemed to ebb out of her and she appeared dull and listless. Because of Fiona's own inner tension she could sympathise wholeheartedly with Judi's and she felt angry with Rowan because of his apparent unconcern. He must know that Judi was in love with him, even though it seemed to amuse him to treat her like a pretty, playful kitten!

'He treats Jenny with far more seriousness than he treats Judi,' Fiona thought a couple of days later as she heard Rowan carefully explaining to her daughter the exact meaning of 'serendipity', a word which she had come across in the book she was reading. Her lips compressed as she saw the way that Jenny, quite unselfconsciously, had climbed on to Rowan's knee. That he was genuinely fond of the little girl she did not doubt, but the knowledge was more pain than pleasure. She found it impossible to forget the baby that had died. Wasn't it possible that Rowan, older now and more mature, would come to feel the need to right an old wrong? Tessa had been under gentle influences and she, too, had changed a great deal in eight years. If by any chance the old attraction revived and Rowan decided to marry her it would not be the hopeless mésalliance that once it would have been. . . .

Jenny, tired of reading, had scrambled down from Rowan's lap and at his suggestion had rushed off into the garden to chase the leaves that were drifting down from the trees to make a carpet of brown and gold. Rowan came to stand by Fiona.

'Fiona, don't you think that as you're staying here until after Christmas you ought to do something about sending Jenny to school? She seems to be very well advanced for her age, but she oughtn't to miss a whole term's work, surely? Apart from any other consideration she needs the companionship of other children.'

He paused, then added with a slightly crooked smile, 'Forgive me if you think I'm being impossibly interfering. I do have Jenny's interests at heart, you know. I'm not just being awkward and officious—at least, I hope I'm not.'

Fiona said slowly, 'It's nice of you to bother about her, Rowan, and I do think you're right. I must admit I've been a bit worried myself. It didn't seem to matter too much when I thought we were only going to be here for a few weeks, but as we're going to stay until after Christmas . . . I'll see if the village school can take her, I think. That will be the best thing.'

'I'm sure that's a wise decision,' Rowan told her. 'Miss Mackenzie—she's the present headmistress—is a very pleasant woman and I have a feeling that she and Jenny will probably take to each other on sight. It's only a small school, as you know, but the standards are very high.'

'I don't know whether Jenny will take too kindly to the idea at first,' Fiona said a little ruefully. 'She's enjoying her long holiday. On the other hand, she has missed having playmates of her own age.'

'There's always Robbie MacGregor,' Rowan said casually. 'Why not invite him to come and play with Jenny? I know he's quite a bit older, but they seemed to get on very well together the other day.'

Fiona stiffened. 'No!' The word was out before she could stop it and she saw the look of astonishment that crossed Rowan's face.

'Why ever not?' Then, as she did not answer, 'Don't you think that a crofter's son is a suitable playmate for the Laird's granddaughter?'

Fiona flushed hotly. 'That makes no difference at all!'

'I'm glad to hear it. Neil was always a ghastly snob,

but you never used to be one, Fiona.' Then, as she bit her lip, ' Robbie's a fine little boy and I have nothing but profound sympathy and admiration for Tessa. She's got pluck and resolution and she's made something out of her life despite a distinctly shaky start. She—what on earth is the matter? What have I said now?'

Fiona had risen to her feet, white and trembling. ' Nothing. I—I think I can hear Jenny calling me. Excuse me!' and she fled, leaving Rowan staring after her, his brows knit together in a startled frown.

Fiona had never felt so angry in all her life. How Rowan had the incredible nerve to accuse her of snobbery, invite her to share his admiration for Tessa's courage, when all the time it was he who—oh, it was despicable of him! She would never have believed him capable of such appalling hypocrisy!

She was still flaming with indignation when later that day Judi rushed into the kitchen, where Fiona was preparing a supper tray for Jenny, and announced that Rowan was taking her for a drive.

' Can I borrow your headscarf, please, Fiona? I need one, it's blowing half a gale, but I can't find mine anywhere,' she said breathlessly.

' Of course. Help yourself.' Fiona did not look up, but she made a private resolution to go to bed early. If Rowan was taking Judi for a drive he would probably come in for a cup of coffee when he brought her back and she, Fiona, had no wish to see him!

She was, in fact, undressing for bed when she heard the sound of wheels on gravel. She looked out of the window just in time to see Judi hurrying into the house from Rowan's car and her brows drew together in a startled frown. Was there some reason why Rowan had brought Judi back so early? He had not got out of the car to open the door for her and he drove away very fast, without even a backward look or a casual salute.

A few moments later she heard the sound of Judi's footsteps, followed by a bang as she slammed her bedroom door. Fiona hesitated, then decided, somewhat reluctantly, that she ought to investigate.

There was no answer to her tentative rap and her 'May I come in, please, Judi?' so she drew a deep breath, turned the handle, and went in.

The room was in darkness and when Fiona switched on the light she saw Judi lying face downwards on the bed, fully clothed. Her face was pressed into her pillows and her slender, graceful body was shaking with sobs.

'Judi! Oh, my dear, whatever is it?' Fiona exclaimed. She almost ran across the room, sat down on the edge of the bed, and laid her hand gently on Judi's heaving shoulders. 'What's happened? What's upset you? Is it . . . Rowan?'

Judi was crying too hard to have answered even if she'd wanted to. It was some time before the storm of sobs began to slacken and she raised her tear-drenched face to gasp hysterically, 'I hate Rowan! I hate him, do you hear? I never want to see him again!'

Fiona felt her blood run cold. 'Judi! My dear, you don't mean that! You've told me so many times that—'

'I do mean it! I *do*!' Judi sat up and mopped her streaming eyes with a wisp of a handkerchief. 'I hate him! He's a beast, a brute! If I'd ever known what he was really like—oh, *Fiona*!' and she dissolved again into another flood of tears.

Tight-lipped, Fiona stared down at her. 'I—I don't understand, Judi. What happened tonight?

133

Why did Rowan bring you home so early? What has he done to make you feel so angry with him?'

Judi went on crying, noisily, hopelessly. Fiona, feeling almost desperate, went into the bathroom to fetch her a glass of water. When she returned Judi had somehow regained a measure of self-control, but she still looked so white and distressed that Fiona's heart went out to her.

'Drink this, Judi dear, and don't cry any more. No man is worth it—and especially not Rowan!' She regretted the last four words directly she had spoken them, but it was too late to call them back.

'Don't I know it!' Judi's voice was hard as she dabbed again at her swollen eyes. Then, as Fiona opened her mouth to speak, 'I'm all right now, thanks, Fiona. Don't say anything to Aunt or Uncle about this and please, *please* don't ask me any questions! I —I don't want to talk about what's happened! I—I *can't*!'

'But, Judi—' Fiona stopped, biting her lip. She couldn't force Judi's confidence. And didn't she know enough about Rowan to guess what had probably happened, anyway?

'Heartbreaker!' Someone had once called Rowan that in the old days. It had been a joke, then, and everyone had laughed. Now, Fiona thought bitterly as she returned to her bedroom, it was no longer a joke. Or if it was there were at least three women—herself, Tessa and now Judi—who could scarcely be expected to find it in the least amusing.

Judi was very pale but otherwise outwardly normal when she appeared at breakfast-time the next morning. Fiona, who had a splitting headache as a result of a completely sleepless night, looked far worse, and her

134

appearance would doubtless have been a cause for concerned questioning had Margaret Campbell not been solely preoccupied with her husband. Arrangements had been made for him to be admitted into an Edinburgh nursing home that afternoon and the vital operation was to be performed early the next day.

Judi did not mention Rowan and went off to work immediately she had finished her toast and coffee. Fiona, guessing that her parents-in-law would prefer to spend the morning alone together, decided to pay a visit to the village school in the hope of enrolling Jenny as a pupil. Rather to her surprise Jenny had been wildly enthusiastic about the idea directly it had been put to her.

'It looks such a funny wee school, Mommy! I'd like to do lessons there. And I might make some friends, too. I only know Robbie. He's nice, but I'd quite like to have some girl-friends, too.'

'Then we'll see what we can arrange with Miss Mackenzie. That's the name of the headmistress.'

Jenny shook back her long fair hair. 'Nearly everyone is "Mac" something in Scotland! I wish we weren't just plain Campbell!'

'It's a good old Scottish name,' Fiona told her. 'You should be very proud of it.'

'I am.' Pause. 'If you marry Uncle Steve your name will be Connaught, won't it? Will mine be Connaught, too?'

'No.' Fiona decided to ignore the wider implications of her daughter's question and to give a straightforward answer. 'You'll always be Jenny Campbell.'

'Until I get married,' Jenny pointed out, and danced away to find her mackintosh and boots. It had rained heavily during the night and the sky was still grey and threatening.

The narrow loch road was full of ruts and holes and pools of rainwater brimmed them all. Jenny zig-zagged from one to another, shouting with glee while her mother walked along more sedately. She still had a headache and it was a relief to feel the freshness of the wind as it blew against her face.

The interview at the school was a great success. Miss Mackenzie was a slight, pleasant-faced woman in her early forties who greeted Fiona and Jenny with a friendly smile and who promptly agreed that the latter's education ought not to be further neglected.

Jenny, delighted by the look of the bright, attractive schoolroom with its colour-washed walls and gay friezes, looked eagerly at her new teacher.

'When may I start, please? Next week?'

'Why not this morning?' Miss Mackenzie suggested. 'Look, there's an empty desk over there by the window, next to Sheila. Would you like to sit there? I'll tell you the names of all the other children and by the end of the day I'm sure you'll have made friends.'

Jenny, her eyes sparkling, lost no time in installing herself at the old-fashioned, ink-stained desk that had been used by generations of Invéray children before her. Miss Mackenzie looked at Fiona and laughed.

'That seems to be settled! I hope you don't mind returning home minus a daughter, Mrs Campbell?'

It was not what Fiona had anticipated, but none-theless she was delighted by Jenny's ability to take new experiences in her stride. By the time she left all the children, including Jenny, were happily absorbed in making paper houses, their bright little faces tense with concentration and their small fingers liberally bedaubed with glue.

Walking back alone along the loch road, Fiona knew that she should feel grateful to Rowan for reminding her that much as Jenny was enjoying her holiday, she needed the stimulation of school and playmates. What was it he had said? 'I do have Jenny's interests at heart. . . .'

It was probably true, too, she thought wistfully. He had never made any secret of the fact that he was fond of Jenny. He didn't spoil her—she couldn't accuse him of that—but he always had time to play with her and to talk to her. She sighed. In other circumstances she would probably have been amused and touched by Rowan's *tendresse* for her daughter and the child's answering devotion, but as it was she couldn't help wishing that Jenny was far less attached to her new 'uncle'. She would have to forget all about him when she returned to America, anyway.

Although it was November, many of the trees still carried their leaves. Fiona, lifting her eyes to their dark sculptured beauty, realised with an unpleasant sense of shock that the sky was even more lowering than before. Almost certainly, she thought ruefully, she was going to get caught in a downpour. She began to walk more quickly, but had not covered more than a hundred yards or so before it began to rain really hard.

It was the kind of downpour that makes nonsense of protective clothing, but nonetheless Fiona stopped to fish in the pocket of her scarlet mackintosh for a plastic hood. As she did so a big car slid to a halt beside her with a hush of wet tyres. Her spirits lifted, but almost immediately dropped again as she recognised both car and driver.

The door was pushed open from inside and Rowan's voice said, 'Hop in. No sense in getting soaked to the skin even if you are a braw Scots lassie used to braving the weather at its worst!'

137

Fiona hesitated, but just at that moment she heard the distant rumble of thunder. That decided her. She got in beside him without a word.

'Where's Jenny?' he demanded, letting in the clutch, and then, as Fiona told him, 'Oh, good. I told Miss Mackenzie you'd probably be bringing her along. Nice to know that she's settled down already.'

'Yes. She's pretty adaptable, thank goodness.'

Rowan shot her a quick look. 'It's lucky that she takes after you and not Neil.'

Not wishing to discuss her husband's character—had Rowan known of the weaknesses that Neil had been at such pains to keep hidden? she wondered—Fiona sat silent. She had taken it for granted that Rowan would drive her home to Cragside, but where the road forked he turned the car right, into the narrow lane leading to his own house.

'You can come and have a cup of coffee with me,' he said calmly when Fiona protested. 'Dad's away just now: he's staying with his sister. He's so much better and stronger that when he's here he wants to start doing things. Aunt Marion will soon sort him out if he's at all obstreperous under her roof! I expect you remember her, don't you, Fiona? We used to be terrified of her as kids, though quite honestly I don't think we need have been. Her bark was always very much worse than her bite.'

Fiona laughed in spite of herself. 'Yes, I do remember her. She locked you in your bedroom once and you climbed out of the window and sprained your ankle.'

'I must have been an odious brat! Isn't it lucky that I've turned out moderately well?' Rowan said with mock smugness, and then, shooting her a swift, teasing look, 'Oh, but of course you don't think I have, do you? No one could ever accuse you of being an ardent member of the Rowan Macrae fan club!'

Fiona bit her lip, remembering Judi's despairing sobs of the previous night. Bother the coffee, she ought to have insisted on being driven straight home!

They weren't at Rivendell yet. She said hastily, 'I —I really don't think I ought to stay for coffee, Rowan. I said I wouldn't be long and it's after eleven already.'

'Rubbish. If I hadn't picked you up it would have been another half an hour or more before you got home. Not only that, you'd have been soaking wet,' he said easily.

'Perhaps, but that doesn't alter the fact that I don't *want* any coffee—' she began crossly, but Rowan, turning into the gateway of Rivendell, merely gave her a mocking grin.

'All right. You can sit and watch me drink mine, but I warn you that you'll probably hurt poor Mrs Brady's feelings beyond repair. She rather prides herself on making good coffee.'

Had he always been so autocratic, even as a boy? If he had, she'd never minded—then. For both her and Neil, Rowan's word had been law. Oh, Neil had grumbled sometimes, perhaps, but in the end he'd always done what Rowan wanted. He had, of course, been a much weaker character. What had been determination in Rowan had been stubbornness in Neil and, equally, what had been cool courage in Rowan had been bravado in his friend .

She was wetter than she'd realised. At any rate directly Mrs Brady caught sight of her she gave a horrified exclamation.

'Goodness me, Miss Fiona, I suppose you got caught in the rain? I'll find you a towel to dry your hair and you'd better borrow one of Mr Rowan's sweaters, too.

139

You look half frozen: you'll be taking a chill before we know where we are and that will never do!'

Fiona protested that her mackintosh had kept her dry and that anyway she rarely caught cold, but it was no use.

'You'd better give in gracefully,' Rowan advised her, looking amused. 'Mrs Brady bosses everyone around here, including me!'

'Get along with you, Mr Rowan!' Mrs Brady said, laughing as she handed Fiona a navy-blue sweater.

'Thank you.' Fiona took it reluctantly. It was ridiculous, but as she slipped it over her head she somehow seemed to feel the warmth and substance of the man to whom it belonged.

When she had finished drying her hair Mrs Brady directed her into the study. She found Rowan standing by the window, watching the rain, but directly he heard her footsteps behind him he swung round. There was an odd expression on his face as he looked at her, clad in the too-big sweater with her damp hair curling in soft tendrils around her face, but Fiona did not hear the deep intake of his breath. She was as conscious of his nearness as if he were touching her and it was an effort to appear quite cool and unconcerned.

'Come and sit down. Coffee's poured out already,' he said cheerfully. Then, as Fiona did as she was told, 'Actually I didn't ask you here just to drink a cup of coffee, Fiona, though I made that my excuse. There's something I'd like to give you for Jenny, and I thought that this would probably be as good a chance as any.'

He put his hand into his pocket and drew something out. He opened his fingers and Fiona saw something blue and gold glinting in the palm of his hand.

He said calmly, 'It's a turquoise bracelet which belonged to my mother when she was a little girl.

Originally, I believe, it belonged to her great-grandmother. I happened to come across it the other day and Dad and I both agreed that we'd like Jenny to wear it.'

Fiona stared down at the dainty little bracelet in stunned silence. Jenny would love it, of course she would. What little girl wouldn't? But—

She said slowly, her eyes anywhere but on Rowan's face, 'Rowan, no! I—I can't possibly take it! Not for Jenny. It—you may have daughters of your own one day and then you'll be terribly sorry that you've given such a lovely thing away. After all, it's—it's a family heirloom! It—' She stopped, suddenly unable to go on.

Rowan's voice was very quiet. 'Those daughters of mine are completely mythical at the moment, Fiona. Anyway, I still want Jenny to have this. You see, the first time I saw it, many years ago, I pictured the little girl who'd one day wear it. She looked exactly like Jenny. I was wrong about only one thing. She happens to be Neil's daughter and not mine, but that really doesn't make any difference. I still want her to have it.'

'She's Niel's daughter and not mine. . . .' The words struck at Fiona's heart. Oh, it was too much! She couldn't bear any more! She turned away, blinded by a sudden rush of tears, her lips quivering, and Rowan, his face changing, sprang forward.

'Fiona! Oh, Fiona, my darling, don't cry! I didn't mean—I hoped you'd be pleased—'

His arms went round her, swift and sure, and then, as she lifted her face to his he gave a smothered exclamation and bending his head, kissed her, kissed her hard.

It was so unexpected that Fiona did not have time to

resist. She even responded to the warm pressure of the hard lips on hers. This was where she belonged, in the arms of her love. . . .

Not *her* love! Bitterly ashamed that for even a few seconds she could have forgotten the pain that Rowan had caused by his careless unconcern for women's hearts, Fiona tried to wrench herself free. Instead of immediately releasing her, Rowan kissed her again, more passionately than before. Fiona, terrified by a sensation of melting into him, of identification, reacted in a way she was afterwards bitterly to regret. She raised her hand and hit him across his face, hit him hard.

'Oh, you—you womaniser!' she choked.

There was a deathly silence. Rowan dropped his hands, stepped back and stared at her, and at the change in his face Fiona caught her breath, half afraid.

Very deliberately he put up his hand, touched the red mark across his cheek. 'A little drastic, my dear, however unwelcome my advances. However, I think it may safely be said that I've got the message.'

His voice prickled with sarcasm, but it did not occur to Fiona in her panic-stricken state to wonder whether the sarcasm was merely a cover for an underlying hurt. She said wildly, 'If you're looking for a replacement for Judi you needn't start wondering whether I might do—temporarily, of course, until someone more attractive looms on the horizon! I'm just not vulnerable, Dr Macrae, perhaps because I was inoculated against your charms at a very early age!'

'A replacement for Judi? Rowan stared at her, a deep crease gathering between his brows. Then suddenly, unforgivably, he laughed.

'Fiona, you're surely not mad with me because I had to talk like a Dutch uncle to that infant, are you?

I knew I'd upset her, but there was nothing else I could have done, and anyway she'll get over it, she truly will. What on earth did she tell you to make you so Mrs Grundyish?'

'She told me nothing. She was in no fit state last night to say anything at all.' Fiona's voice shook a little.

'And you blame me for that? Oh, look, Fiona, grow up! You surely don't think that I—'

Fiona thrust her hands down into the pockets of her slacks. 'It doesn't matter what I think, does it?'

Rowan's lips thinned. 'I think it does. I admit I shouldn't have kissed you, Fiona, but—well, what's a kiss between old friends? Nothing to make a fuss about, surely. Most men have their weaker moments, and you need never tell your precious Steve!'

It was too much for Fiona. She said furiously, 'The trouble is that you have more weaker moments than most men, Rowan! What about Tessa, or is that nothing to make a fuss about, too?'

He stood as if turned to stone. Fiona, feeling that she would give a small fortune to be able to take her words back, almost shrank from his steady, unreadable stare. Then he said slowly, 'I think you'd better explain what you mean, Fiona.'

She turned her head away. 'I—I shouldn't have said anything. I—I'm sorry. If you hadn't made me so angry—'

'But you did say something.' The words snapped. 'I want to know what you meant.'

Fiona drew a long breath. Then in a hard, tight little voice she didn't recognise as her own she said, 'I know that you had an affair with Tessa eight years ago. I know you were the father of her baby.' She saw the shock go across his face as if she had hit him again

143

and added swiftly, 'You needn't worry. I—I haven't told anyone else. And I never, never will.'

'You . . . say you know . . . about Tessa and me.' He repeated the words slowly. Then, more sharply, '*How* did you know?'

Fiona moistened her lips. She mustn't let him guess that it was because of his affair with Tessa that she had turned to Neil for comfort. She said carefully, 'Neil told me. After we were married.'

Rowan turned away abruptly. He took several rapid strides away from her and stood facing the window. Then over his shoulder he said coolly, 'And of course it didn't occur to you to wonder whether Neil was telling the truth?'

'No,' she added lamely, 'I was sure he was.'

The silence stretched. After a few seconds Rowan turned and came back to her. His face looked quite impassive.

'Since you've kept quiet about this for eight years I presume you're still willing to hold your tongue?'

Fiona swallowed. 'Of course.'

'I appreciate your consideration.' Rowan's voice was hard. 'And now, if you care to drink your coffee, I'll take you home.'

'Rowan—'

'Jenny's bracelet.' Rowan held it out. 'If you don't wish her to accept it as a gift from me, let her accept it from my father.'

Fiona took the glittering chain wordlessly. It was cold against her fingers and it matched both the coldness in her heart and the coldness she saw in Rowan's dark blue eyes.

CHAPTER IX

Fiona's uneasy conviction that she had allowed herself to be panicked into behaving extremely foolishly was strengthened that evening when Judi asked her if she could borrow an envelope.

'I'd wait until tomorrow and buy some, only I particularly want Rowan to get this letter as soon as possible,' she said, folding a piece of closely-written notepaper. Then, as Fiona raised her brows, she added wryly, 'It's an apology, in case you're interested.'

'An apology? Isn't the boot on the wrong foot? I'd have thought that if there was any apologising to be done—' Fiona began, but Judi interrupted her. A wave of burning colour had washed into her piquant little face.

'I thought you might say something like that. Fiona, I—I ought to explain about last night. I don't know what I said, exactly, but I rather imagine that I probably gave you the impression that—well, that Rowan had been pretty beastly to me.'

She regarded the toe of her shoe fixedly. 'Actually he wasn't beastly at all, not really. It—it isn't fair to let you go on thinking that he was.' She paused and swallowed. 'It isn't very easy for me to say this, but—but I put him in an almost impossible position. I—well, I haven't much excuse except that I suddenly decided that I was fed up with being treated like his favourite kid sister and I couldn't take any more.'

Fiona stared at her. 'I don't think I know what you mean.'

Judi looked acutely embarrassed. 'Oh, Fiona, *don't* make me spell it out! I—I made a bit of an ass of

145

myself and Rowan had to explain that although he was frightfully fond of me and all the rest of it he didn't exactly have anything more definite in mind. I—I knew that really. He's never given me any reason to suppose he'd fallen in love with me, but—but I usually get what I want and—and I couldn't help hoping.'

There was a moment's silence. Then Fiona said slowly, almost disbelievingly, 'Then all those tears—'

'Tears of sheer frustration and bad temper.' Judi gave her a shamefaced grin. 'Bruce is quite right, you know. I *am* horribly spoilt. When people don't do what I want them to do and I can't get my own way I cry and get into a tizz. It must have been rather ghastly for poor Rowan. He did his best to calm me down, but I'm pretty sure he must have been fearfully glad to get rid of me!'

Fiona said nothing. In paying silent tribute to Judi's rueful honesty she could not help realising with intense dismay what Rowan had been trying to tell her. What was it he'd said? Something about having had to talk to Judi like a Dutch uncle. . . . 'I knew I'd upset her, but there was nothing else I could have done, and anyway she'll get over it, truly she will.'

Well, he seemed to be right about that. Now that her first angry outburst was over Judi certainly seemed to bear Rowan very little ill-will and she had already recovered much of her normal ebulllience. It was Fiona, remembering the indignation she had felt on Judi's behalf and the wild accusations she had hurled at Rowan's head, who probably felt the most mortified. She tried to tell herself that it was Rowan's calm assumption that she would welcome his lovemaking, rather than his treatment of Judi, that had triggered off the unpleasant scene that had followed, but despite all her self-justifying arguments she knew that she had made a complete mess of things.

She did not see Rowan again for several days. When she did he was so much a polite stranger that she realised that he was unlikely to forgive her for revealing that she knew of his past indiscretion. The thought gave her a queer, lonely little ache in her heart. Rowan, for all his faults, was—Rowan. In an odd sort of way he was as much a part of the fabric of her life as Jenny. She had believed at one time that she had forgotten all about him, that he no longer mattered, but it simply was not true. He was still in her system, like a dormant fever in her blood. Even when she returned to the States and to Steve she would carry his memory with her.

Judi announced her intention of leaving Inveray when she had finished typing the final draft of John Paterson's new book. Completion, it seemed, was likely in late January or early February. Since she only worked in the mornings she and Fiona were able to take it in turns to accompany Margaret Campbell when she visited her husband in his Edinburgh nursing home. He had stood the long and difficult operation well, but his eyes were heavily bandaged and he was under strict instructions to move as little as possible. As a result he found time hanging heavily upon his hands and he eagerly looked forward to visits from his friends and family.

On a number of occasions Bruce tore himself away from his other duties to act as chauffeur, and Fiona, who had decided on their first meeting that here was a man one could both admire and respect, found herself liking him more and more. She had a shrewd suspicion that Judi, too, was regarding him in a new and more favourable light. At any rate she had stopped talking about him, which Fiona felt was a very good sign. She had babbled endlessly about Rowan just as a child might babble about a coveted toy which, once obtained, immediately lost the greater part of its attraction. She had never really been in love with him. Fiona felt sure of that. As Bruce had so shrewdly observed, her infatuation for him had been a legacy from her childhood, when he and Nail had been her idols and she had been content to be their willing slave.

At any rate, when Bruce happened to comment on the fact that Rowan's visits to Cragside had become increasingly infrequent, Fiona had no hesitation in putting him in the picture. She was careful not to give Judi away, but she did make it clear that the younger girl was no longer regarding Rowan in the light of a possible husband.

' Just as well. He's the wrong man for her,' Bruce observed. Then, with the ghost of a smile, ' I suppose I would say that, wouldn't I? But—my own feelings apart—I think I'm right.'

' Yes, I agree.'

Bruce looked at her, a rueful smile curving his lips. ' I love Judi very much. I think you've guessed that. Do you think I stand a chance?'

His eyes were anxious, but he stood like a rock, tall, strong and undeniably attractive. Fiona smiled at him.

' I don't see why not. You've certainly overcome her initial—er—prejudices. But don't try and rush her, Bruce.'

' I won't. At least I've got a clear field. Judi's never looked at anyone besides Macrae.' He paused, then added casually, ' Incidentally, do you think she knows that tongues are wagging over him and Miss Mac-Gregor?'

148

Fiona went white. She couldn't help it. 'What do you mean?'

He shot her a surprised glance. 'Nothing, really. You know what it's like in a small village. No man can be seen in the company of a pretty girl without someone beginning to wonder if romance is brewing. In this case, I gather, there's more than the usual amount of interest. I don't know why.'

Fiona, who did, said with forced calmness, 'Tessa is the local girl who made good. And—and she's very beautiful.'

'She certainly is.' Bruce, despite the fact that his affections were otherwise engaged, spoke with unusual enthusiasm and Fiona was conscious of an odd little pang. If even Bruce was struck by Tessa's beauty, what about Rowan? 'Perhaps she's always been in his blood, just as he has been in mine, and that's why he's never married,' she thought. Well, Tessa had somehow managed to live down the old scandal. If she and Rowan decided to get married now there'd be very few raised eyebrows or spiteful whispers. Anyway, Rowan was not planning to stay in Inveray permanently. It was common knowledge that old Dr Macrae was hoping to be able to return to work in the early spring. Rowan would then be free to take a job anywhere—Edinburgh, Glasgow, Aberdeen or even further afield. Anywhere where Tessa's story would not be known. . . .

Fiona had not realised, until Rowan's visits to Cragside became few and far between, how much she would miss them and the stimulation of his company. On the surface, however, her life continued much as before, with just a little undercurrent of vague pain and dissatisfaction running through it whenever she thought about the man whose eyes, whenever he looked at her, were as cold and as bleak as the North Sea. She was haunted by a sense of 'something gone that should be there', but she was reluctant to admit that this was caused by the change in Rowan's attitude towards her. It simply wasn't sensible, and surely, at twenty-eight, one was sensible if nothing else.

Luckily no one else seemed to have noticed Rowan's cold formality. In a way, Fiona thought, things had worked out quite well. Everyone seemed to take it for granted that the reason Rowan stayed away from Cragside was because his friendship with Judi had cooled and because Douglas Campbell, who had been his patient, was now under hospital care. Nobody, except Rowan and herself, knew of the violent break that had occurred on that wet and windy day at Rivendell.

With Jenny at school—and rapidly establishing herself as a star pupil—Fiona devoted most of her time to her mother-in-law, but when the weather permitted she also did a little sketching. On impulse she sent one of her best efforts—a black and white drawing of a roebuck in the glen—to Steve Connaught. She didn't quite know why, except that she was feeling a little guilty about him. As she had expected, he had been very upset by the news that she intended to prolong her holiday and had written her a great many wild and whirling words to the effect that not only was he missing her unbearably but that he strongly suspected that she was being 'emotionally blackmailed' by the Campbells.

Fiona had promptly sent him a somewhat tart response and the sketch of the roebuck was in the nature of a peace-offering. She hoped he would recognise it as such. He had been kind to her and she owed him a lot. She could not—would not!—allow the ridiculous way she felt about Rowan to affect a friendship

150

which before her return to Inveray she had enjoyed and even valued.

Nevertheless, she was surprised and also considerably dismayed when a few days later she received an airmail letter from Steve stating that he had to make an unexpected business trip to London before Christmas and would like to come and see her. Could she please recommend a good local hotel where he could stay for a few days?

'I do have a few misgivings, for I realise that one should never make one's first visit to Scotland in the depths of winter, but I'm hoping that the warmth of your welcome will dispel most of the climatic chilliness I'm told to expect!' Steve wrote in his rather pompous way. 'I'm longing to see you again and also —I must be truthful—to satisfy myself that you really are staying on in Inveray from a sense of duty and not from inclination. . . .'

Fiona stared down at the letter for a long time after reading it. Steve's request was a complication she had certainly not foreseen. Did she want him here at Inveray and, if she did, how would he fit in? Despite the assurance that Douglas Campbell had given her, would he and his wife welcome the presence of a stranger who would almost certainly make no secret of the fact that he hoped to marry their idolised son's widow?

In the end, somewhat diffidently, she broached the matter to her mother-in-law and was relieved by her reaction.

'Mr Connaught? I think I've heard a little about him from Jenny, haven't I?' Then, as Fiona flushed, 'If he's coming all this way to see you why not invite him to stay here, Fiona? Goodness only knows we've got plenty of room and he'll feel more at home, perhaps, than he would in a hotel.'

'You're sure you wouldn't . . . mind?'

'Of course not, my dear.' Margaret Campbell hesitated, then added, 'It's nice to see a new face occasionally. I'd very much like to meet Mr Connaught and so would Douglas, I'm sure.'

'Then I'll write to Steve straight away,' Fiona said, and wondered why she felt such a lack of enthusiasm. Her feelings, she later discovered, were shared by her daughter.

'Uncle Steve coming here? But why, Mommy? He belongs in the States,' she protested.

'So do we,' Fiona said quickly, and then immediately regretted her words, for Jenny looked mutinous.

'We belong here too! I like Scotland better than the States! I wish we could stay here, for ever and for ever!'

'Oh, Jenny!' Fiona checked a rueful laugh. 'You know quite well we can't do that!'

'Why can't we? Granny and Grandpapa want us to stay!'

'Yes, but—' Fiona stopped helplessly. How could she explain the way she felt to Jenny, when she couldn't even begin to explain it to herself? How could she tell Jenny that because Rowan had never been to America he'd left no ghosts and there was nothing there that could hurt her? Here at Inveray unfading echoes of her lost love were all about her: nearly every spot she looked upon held some bitter-sweet memory.

Jenny tugged insistently at her sleeve. 'Do you want to be with Uncle Steve? Is that why we've got to go back to the States? Is he coming here to collect us?'

'No, darling. I've told you, he's got business in London. He's just going to pay us a short visit.'

152

'How short?'

'I really don't know. You ask far too many questions, my poppet.' Fiona tried hard not to feel exasperated by the child's persistence.

Unexpectedly Jenny chuckled. 'So did you when you were a little girl. Uncle Rowan told me.'

'When?' Fiona asked sharply.

'Yesterday. You know you let me go and play with Robbie after school? Well, he came to see Miss Mac-Gregor about something. He stayed quite a long time.'

'Oh, I see.' Fiona caught her lower lip between her teeth. Although Duncan MacGregor had been discharged from hospital and was well on the road to complete recovery, it seemed that his daughter was in no hurry to return to Glasgow.

Jenny leaned against her. Fiona put her arm round her small shoulders and looked down at her. Jenny returned her smile.

'Mommy, I do look like you, don't I?'

'So people say.'

'Miss MacGregor thinks I'm like Daddy, too. She told Uncle Rowan that when I'm cross about something I scowl just like Daddy used to. Nobody's ever told me that before.'

Fiona was conscious of a faint sense of shock. It was true. Jenny's rare scowl had always had a vaguely familiar quality, but until now she had never realised why. How odd it was that Tessa, who had never known Neil very well, had been quick to spot a resemblance which had apparently escaped everyone else!

Now she said cheerfully, 'Well, you don't scowl very often, I hope. What made you cross yesterday?'

'Robbie. He wouldn't let me hold his hamster. Sometimes he's awfully mean, Mommy, but I still like him better than anyone else.'

That was the way she'd felt about Rowan at Jenny's age, Fiona thought, and sighed. One grew out of one's childish attachments. Or one should. Why couldn't she wake up one morning and find that Rowan no longer mattered to her? Why did he still have the power to hurt her? It wasn't fair, when she'd tried so hard for eight years to forget him, to find that she was as emotionally vulnerable as ever!

Judi came into the room humming a tune from the film musical she'd seen the previous evening with Bruce. She looked her old gay, sparkling self. Why couldn't she be more like Judi? Fiona wondered. There was nothing at all to indicate that the younger girl was suffering from a broken heart. In fact, it seemed that she had already reached the stage when she could look back on her infatuation for Rowan with a kind of rueful amusement.

'Fiona, do you or do you not realise it's nearly Christmas?' she demanded, draping herself gracefully over the arm of a chair. 'It will be a white one if we're lucky. Angus told me this morning that he's sure we'll have snow extra early this year, and you know what a famous weather prophet he is!'

Fiona raised her brows. 'You're not returning to London to spend Christmas with your parents, then?'

'No. They're going off on a cruise. They invited me to join them, actually, but I'd much rather stay here. I like old-fashioned Christmases, with holly and yule logs and carols and hot punch and children's parties. You'll have one for Jenny, of course?'

Fiona hesitated, then nodded. In the old days the Campbells had always given a party for the children of the clachan and Margaret had already suggested that this year the practice might be renewed. It would be hard work for everyone, but Jenny would probably be thrilled to bits.

Judi's dark eyes sparkled. ' Oh, good! We'll have to rope in either Bruce or Rowan to play Santa Claus. Unless your Steve would like the job, Fiona? He'll be here for Christmas, too, won't he?'

' Yes, he will.'

' Nice for both of you. I'm simply longing to meet him,' Judi said gaily, and did not see the shadow which had fallen over Fiona's face at the mention of Steve's name.

Angus's prophecy proved correct. There was a light sprinkling of snow during the next two days and this was followed by a really heavy fall which clothed the glen overnight in a thick mantle of pure white snow-blossom.

Douglas Campbell, on his way home to Cragside from his Edinburgh nursing home, could not appreciate the wonderful glitter of sun on frost because of his heavily tinted spectacles. Neverthless he was fully aware that 'tide of whiteness covered the dark earth that he loved and he smiled to himself, a smile of pure contentment. The operation had been successful. His eyesight would never be good and he would always have to guard against strain or excessive fatigue, but at least there was no longer any fear that he was doomed to live in a world of perpetual darkness. He felt, as the car whirled him through the snowy landscape, like a man reborn.

At Cragside his family and a few close friends, including Rowan and his father, were waiting to greet him. The big hall had been decorated with holly and mistletoe and evergreens from the woods, and a huge tree sparkled with fairy lights and multi-coloured baubles. It was a festive scene and a festive occasion, and no one seemed gayer than Fiona, whose coral dress made a vivid splash of colour and whose flushed cheeks and sparkling eyes vied, for once, with Judi's. She tried very hard to ignore Rowan's tall, broad, debonair presence, but unfortunately for her her daughter had quite different ideas.

'Look, Uncle Rowan! I'm wearing the bracelet you gave me!' Jenny, standing by her mother's side, triumphantly extended a slender brown wrist as Rowan came up to them. 'Doesn't it look lovely?'

'Very pretty,' Rowan assured her, smiling. His eyes, chilling until they were as cold as grey agates, found Fiona's. 'I'm glad you're allowing her to wear it.'

'Of course. She's very proud of it.' Fiona answered him lightly, but felt a pang of dismay as Jenny darted across the room to meet Bruce, a late arrival.

Rowan's gaze travelled slowly over her. She found nothing reassuring in his steady scrutiny even though he said coolly, 'You look even more beautiful than your daughter. You should wear vivid colours far more often, Fiona. They suit you.' Then, before she could answer, 'Incidentally, did you know that the clasp of your necklace is undone? I'll fasten it for you.'

In spite of herself Fiona shivered as his warm strong fingers brushed her bare neck. He must have felt her involuntary recoil because for a moment something showed in his face that might have been anger.

'Don't worry, Fiona. There are enough people here tonight to ensure your complete safety,' he said bitingly.

'I—I don't know what you mean.'

'I think you do.' He smiled, but his eyes were unamused. 'You made it very clear the other day what you thought of my—er—moral character.

Womaniser—wasn't that the charming expression you used?'

Fiona caught her breath. 'Rowan, I—I'm sorry about that, I really am. If—if I hadn't been feeling so worried about Judi—' She stopped, following the direction of Rowan's gaze. Judi, her face alight with mischief and laughter, was standing under a sprig of mistletoe, beckoning towards Bruce.

'I think your worry was a little misplaced, don't you?' Rowan's voice was sardonic. 'Judi was never in love with me and I knew that right from the very first. It was only a childish fancy. I told you that, and now perhaps you'll believe me.'

'Yes, I do. But—' Fiona stopped, unable to go on.

'But that still leaves us with Tessa, doesn't it?' Rowan stuck his hands into the pockets of his well cut dinner jacket. 'I wonder, my dear, if you've ever really understood the force of passion and the lengths it can drive you to? I doubt it. Neil was such a paragon of virtue, wasn't he? How lucky that you married him and not me!'

A curious kind of bitterness edged his words. Fiona opened her mouth to utter a stinging retort, but even as she did so the memory of that strange message she had found among Neil's possessions flashed into her mind. Somehow, for some reason, it silenced the hot angry words that trembled on her lips.

For a moment she and Rowan stared at each other in an aching silence. A muscle twitched in the man's cheek. There was a grim tight look about his mouth that baffled and hurt her, but otherwise his expression was as unreadable as a chance-met stranger's.

Impulsively Fiona stretched out her hand. 'Rowan—'

He seemed not to notice her gesture, for he turned

157

away. Over his shoulder he said, 'It's still snowing hard. Your friend Steve is supposed to arrive the day after tomorrow, isn't he? Too bad if he finds himself held up by a raging blizzard. I'm sure you can hardly wait until he gets here.'

Fiona watched him walk across the room and join his father and Douglas Campbell, who were deep in conversation. As he brushed past the Christmas tree it quivered and shook and a silver bauble that must have been insecurely tied fell to the ground and shattered into a thousand tiny fragments. It seemed, to Fiona, to be strangely symbolic.

CHAPTER X

It was snowing hard when Steve Connaught arrived at Inveray, but if the weather was unfriendly he certainly had no reason to complain about the warmth of his welcome. Douglas and Margaret Campbell greeted him with hospitable friendliness and he was soon ensconced in a comfortable armchair with a glass of Douglas Campbell's best brandy in his hand and a yule log blazing on the wide hearth in front of him.

Only Jenny greeted the new arrival with a touch of reserve in her manner. Fiona noticed it and sighed inwardly. There was no doubt about it, Jenny didn't really like Steve. Lissa had declared that the child's attitude was nothing to worry about, but Fiona had always had strong misgivings. What bothered her most was that it didn't seem as though it was a simple case of jealousy. Jenny actually welcomed the idea of a stepfather, but it was pretty obvious that she didn't think that Steve Connaught was a suitable candidate!

'He's nice, Fiona, but surely just a shade too old for you?' Judi, talking to Fiona in the privacy of her bedroom that night, spoke with her usual frankness. 'He's a bit . . . well, staid, isn't he?'

Fiona laughed a little ruefully. 'I suppose he is, but he isn't really all that old, Judi. He's only forty-three.'

'Then there are fifteen years between you. It's a big gap,' Judi argued.

'I don't think so, but anyway you're talking as though our marriage is a foregone conclusion, Judi. It isn't. For one thing Jenny isn't keen on the idea, though I don't know why. Steve has always been very kind to her.'

Judi grinned. 'Ask her if she'd like Rowan for a stepfather and see what her reaction is! She's nearly as crazy about him as I used to be.' She clasped her hands behind her curly dark head. 'Pity you're not interested, Fiona. I no longer want the dear man for myself, but I wouldn't mind keeping him in the family, so to speak!'

The colour flamed into Fiona's face. 'What utter nonsense you talk, Judi!'

'I suppose I do,' Judi admitted calmly. She yawned and stretched. 'Well, don't worry too much. Uncle and Aunt seem to like Steve and I'm sure they'll think that he'll make you a suitable husband. He couldn't be much more of a contrast to Neil, though, could he? Honestly, Fiona, I sometimes wonder—' She stopped abruptly and flushed scarlet.

Fiona stared at her. 'Wonder what? Go on, Judi.'

'Wonder what on earth you ever saw in Neil!' Judi said in a burst of confidence. 'Oh, I know he was my cousin and you shouldn't speak ill of the dead and all that, but—but he simply wasn't *straight*, was he?'

Fiona's brows drew together in a bewildered frown. 'Not straight? I don't think I know what you mean, Judi.'

Judi looked unaccountably embarrassed. She hesitated as if trying to make up her mind what to say, but just at that moment Jenny, in the adjoining bedroom, stirred and called out 'Mommy?' in a drowsy voice.

'Coming, darling.' Fiona went quickly to her daughter's side and by the time she had fetched the drink of water that Jenny wanted and tucked her up again she had almost forgotten what Judi had said. Almost. For some reason she remembered it again when she woke in the middle of the night.

'Not straight. Not straight. Not straight.' The words echoed over and over again in her troubled mind until at last, in sheer desperation, she switched on her bedside lamp and began to read. It was a book that she had picked at random from the library shelves and it did not really interest her, but anything, at the moment, was preferable to thinking about Neil. Neil, who had been her childhood friend, like Rowan, and then her husband. Neil, who had certainly had a darker side to his character than before her marriage she had ever dreamed. . . .

Steve's stay at Cragside was quite pleasant for all concerned. Margaret and Douglas Campbell genuinely liked the big bluff American, and Steve, for his part, seemed greatly impressed both by their hospitality and by his first taste of a real family Christmas.

On Christmas Day the whole household went to church. There was holly everywhere in the tiny kirk and tall, glowing candles shone on the bright red berries and on the greenery that softened the ancient grey stone. Rowan and his father were also at the service and were later introduced to Steve, who, as the only stranger present, was the cynosure of all eyes.

Steve and Rowan didn't take to each other. Fiona realised that immediately, but was at a loss to understand the emotional undercurrents.

'Have you known that Macrae fellow long?' Steve demanded jealously when they returned to Cragside. 'You've never mentioned him in any of your letters.'

'I practically grew up with him,' Fiona said lightly, adding, as Steve frowned, 'We used to be quite good pals, but we haven't a great deal in common now, I'm afraid.'

Steve's handsome face cleared. The following day,

when Rowan and his father came to lunch, he chatted quite affably to them both and even applauded Rowan's jovial appearance as Father Christmas at Jenny's party. Fiona herself gave a creditable impression of enjoyment. No one would have guessed, as she laughed and chatted with the small guests who crowded round her, that she carried a heavy heart.

'The loch is frozen over. Did you know, Mrs Campbell?' Robbie MacGregor asked eagerly. 'Dad thinks the ice will be thick enough for skating quite soon.'

Fiona was conscious of a rush of almost unbearable nostalgia. How many times in the past had she and Rowan gone skating on the loch, flying away together over the dark and ringing ice? Her eyes met Rowan's and a queer, darting, flame-like look passed between them before each turned their head away. Fiona's breath quickened. Perhaps Rowan remembered, too. Perhaps. . . .

'Will you teach me how to skate, please, Mommy?' Jenny asked eagerly.

'*I* will.' Robbie grinned at her. 'It's really quite easy.'

'Tomorrow?' Jenny demanded excitedly.

'No, you must wait until the ice is really firm,' Fiona told her, and then, as her face betrayed her disappointment, 'You wouldn't like to fall through, would you?'

Margaret Campbell appeared, to hand out multicoloured balloons, and the party was over. Steve later found Fiona clearing up the debris in the kitchen and promptly offered to help.

'It will be a treat to have five minutes alone with you,' he said, picking up a tea towel. 'I've found you elusive, Fiona. I like each and every member of the Campbell clan, but they're a little ubiquitous, aren't they?'

Fiona coloured. She had deliberately avoided being left alone with Steve simply because she knew that at the first opportunity he would try to pressurise her into fixing a date for her return to America.

She did not answer and Steve moved towards her. Before she had realised what he intended to do he put his arms around her and stooped to kiss her mouth. When, after a moment, he released her, she stood in the circle of his arms, unhappily wondering how she could tell him that she now knew—had known for the past few weeks—that she could not possibly marry him. She had become wife to one man when her heart had belonged to another: she could not afford to make the same mistake again.

A movement in the doorway caught her eye and she turned her head quickly, a wave of colour flooding into her face as she saw Rowan leaning nonchalantly against the jamb. Enraged by his sardonic expression, she jerked herself free from Steve's embrace and put up her hand to smooth her hair.

All the old hateful mockery was back in Rowan's eyes as he strolled forward.

' I came to help with the washing up,' he said coolly. ' I didn't realise that there wasn't exactly a shortage of—er—volunteers. Still, the more the merrier, isn't that how the saying goes?' and without waiting for an answer he picked up another tea-towel.

Fiona knew that she should feel furious with him. Instead she felt a sneaking relief that the inevitable showdown with Steve had once more been postponed. She didn't want to hurt him, she told herself unhappily as she turned on the hot water tap. Then she glanced at his stony face and realised that she already had, by not letting Rowan know that he was decidedly *de trop.* It would have been quite easy to do.

Half an hour later Jenny made things ten times worse by throwing her arms round Rowan's neck and kissing him goodnight, though she merely smiled politely at Steve. Fiona saw Steve's lips tighten and wished despairingly that she had had the courage to tell him not to come to Inveray. It was hopeless. You couldn't love to order . . . nobody could.

Rowan caught her alone just after she had put Jenny to bed, his tall form barring the way to the door.

' I suppose you think I owe you an apology, Fiona?'

Fiona raised her eyebrows, striving for calm. ' An apology? Whatever for?'

His grey eyes were intimidating. ' For bursting in on that tender little scene earlier this evening, of course. Not that I was altogether to blame. It never occurred to me that with all the other opportunities that are doubtless open to him Connaught would find the aftermath of a children's party a suitable occasion for a spot of lovemaking.' Then, with gentle mockery, ' I'm sure he's a very worthy gentleman, but I can't say I'm particularly impressed by his technique!'

Fiona shot him an angry glance. ' Your own, of course, is so much more effective!'

' Not with you, it isn't.' Rowan paused, his brown face becoming suddenly grim. ' Fiona, are you seriously contemplating getting married to Connaught?'

The unexpectedness of the question took her completely by surprise. In her confusion she forgot that he had no right to ask it. She even tried to prevaricate.

' I—I don't know. I haven't made up my mind.'

' It wouldn't work. You're just not right for each other, Fiona. It sticks out a mile. Even Jenny can see it.'

Fiona stared at him almost disbelievingly. Then

bitterly she said, 'What makes you think *you* know what's right for me and what isn't? What gives *you* the right to dole out advice?'

He drew a deep breath and she saw his lips tighten. 'Because, Fiona, old friendships and old loyalties mean rather more to me than they do to you. Strangely enough, I genuinely care about you and what happens to you. No doubt you think that's presumptuous of me and God knows I've tried not to care, especially after discovering what you really think of me.' He smiled a little grimly as he added, 'Unfortunately one isn't always in a position to dictate these things.'

Fiona could find no immediate words. She felt confused and breathless. 'I—I—'

'If I'm embarrassing you I'm sorry. I won't bring the matter up again. Just . . . be careful, Fiona. Try not to make another bad mistake.'

'M-mistake?'

Rowan's eyes seemed to probe into her mind. He said slowly, as if weighing every word, 'I think you made a mistake when you married Neil, Fiona. You weren't happy with him, were you?' Then, as she made to speak, 'No, don't bother to deny it. Don't ask me how I know, either. I just do.'

'I suppose you imagine that I would have been very much happier with you, whether you were unfaithful to me or not!' she said wildly, and had the satisfaction of seeing his expression change. At least that particular stone had found its mark, she thought, and waited a little apprehensively for the stinging rejoinder he was bound to make.

'I think so, yes. You see, although you seem to find it difficult to believe, I did love you, Fiona.'

'As you loved . . . Tessa?'

Rowan's eyes seemed to harden when she said that.

'I never loved Tessa.'

Fiona looked at him. Then she said angrily, 'In that case Tessa has even more to forgive you for than I thought!'

'Suppose we leave that little matter to her? There are some people, you know, who *can* forget and forgive. Luckily Tessa happens to be one of them.'

'How nice for you! After ruining her life—'

'Tessa's life is not ruined.' There was a cutting edge to his voice. 'I'm glad to say she hasn't lost her chance of happiness. There's an old proverb, you know—better late than never.'

Fiona didn't ask him what he meant. She didn't have to. There was a painful silence, broken at last by the sound of Steve's voice calling, 'Fiona! Fiona, where are you?'

Rowan gave her a mocking glance, then turned away. 'It might be as well if Connaught didn't find us together. He's already suspicious of me, or haven't you noticed?' Then, as she did not answer, 'It's a pity he doesn't know how little he need worry, isn't it? Goodnight, Fiona.'

He went quickly out of the room. Fiona stood motionless for several seconds, then walked slowly to the window. Coldly despairing, she watched Rowan's departure.

'I genuinely care about you and what happens to you. . . .' Had he really spoken those words or had she simply imagined them? Either way it didn't really matter, she thought bitterly. Rowan Macrae was not for her. She could never tell him that she, too, cared. Nothing had changed. Rowan was still guilty concerning Tessa, and the old barrier . . . the barrier that had separated them once before . . . still stood between them.

Two days passed, two difficult days for Fiona because Steve, with the stubbornness of a man unwilling to relinquish something he had believed to be almost within his grasp, refused to accept the fact that although she intended to return to America she had definitely decided not to marry him.

'Why?' he demanded, running his hands through his thick, prematurely grey hair. '*Why?*' Then, as she looked at him despairingly, 'It's nonsense to say that it's because you don't love me. The kind of affection we've always had for each other is as good a foundation for marriage as anything else I know. We could be very happy in a quiet sort of way. After all, where there's a violent attraction there's often conflict as well. Surely you realise that, Fiona?'

Oh yes, thought Fiona, she did. Only too well. . . .

She sat with her head downbent, twisting her handkerchief between her fingers, and Steve eyed her sharply.

'You're sure there's no one else? Because if there is—'

Fiona shook her head. She couldn't possibly explain to Steve the way she felt about Rowan. In any case it was unlikely that he would understand. He was basically a simple, straightforward person. Complexities . . . the solemn secrets of a woman's heart . . . were beyond him.

'I'm sorry, Steve. Please forgive me,' was all she managed to say.

'There's nothing to forgive.' Steve rose to his feet, big and purposeful. 'I don't intend to admit defeat yet, Fiona. When you're back in the States I think it's very likely that you'll feel quite differently about things. You shouldn't have come home to Inveray. I knew at the time it was a mistake.'

A mistake? No, Fiona thought passionately. By returning to Inveray—and Rowan—she had actually been saved from making a mistake. If she had stayed in America she might, for the second time, have been tempted into marrying without love. Perhaps Steve was right and it *was* possible, in certain circumstances, to be happy without the passion of love, but it was wiser not to risk it. Much wiser.

Greatly to her relief Steve was sensible enough not to allow the rebuff she had given him to spoil his enjoyment of the remainder of his visit. It continued to freeze hard, and two days after Jenny's party Fiona yielded to her pleas and agreed to take her down to the loch, where skating was in full swing.

It was a diamond day—clear, cold, hard and brilliant. The sharp blue sky shone, the white hills glittered, and the gaunt bare trees that fringed the loch were black and skeletal in the pale sunlight. Fiona had tied a bright red scarf round her daughter's neck and pulled a red tam o'shanter firmly down on her fair head, though Jenny was far too excited about the prospect of learning to skate to worry overmuch about frozen fingers or toes.

' Oh, look! There's Robbie!' she exclaimed, waving vigorously at one of perhaps a dozen children who thronged the ice. ' Oh, and there's Miss MacGregor!'

Tessa, slim and lithe in navy blue trews and a matching anorak, came smilingly up to them. Her lovely red-gold hair was tied back with a wide ribbon and she looked flushed and sparkling.

' I didn't feel too sure that the ice was really safe, so I thought I'd better come down to see for myself before I let Robbie loose on it,' she said smilingly. ' I think it's all right, though, don't you?'

' Well, even if it isn't I very much doubt whether

168

even wild horses would drag those children away from it now!' Steve observed. His eyes dwelt on Tessa with unconscious appreciation and she did indeed look very beautiful.

Fiona smiled at her. 'Did you have a nice Christmas, Tessa?'

'Marvellous, thanks.' There was a lilt to Tessa's soft voice which made Fiona look at her rather more sharply. There was something about her lovely face—a kind of shining radiance—which suddenly caused a chill thrust of apprehension to run through her.

'I saw your father in church on Christmas Day and thought how well he looked. You'll be able to go back to Glasgow soon, I suppose, Tessa?' She forced herself to ask the question casually, as though the answer did not matter to her one way or the other.

'No.' Tessa's eyes sparkled. 'I'm staying here, in Inveray. Haven't you heard? I'm going to be Dr Macrae's receptionist. It's something I'll love doing, for a little while, at least—I've got other plans for the spring,' she added smilingly.

Other plans. . . . It was easy to guess what they were. Fiona felt a terrible aching hopelessness and she shivered involuntarily. Steve, standing by her side, looked at her with quick concern.

'Are you cold, my dear?'

'I am a bit,' Fiona admitted. 'I shall soon warm up when I'm on the ice, though.'

Tessa took the hint and moved away. Watched by Steve, who was unable to skate and who had no wish to provide amusement for a crowd by learning with Jenny, Fiona gave her daughter some preliminary instruction, finding to her delight that the child grasped the rudiments very quickly. After a comparatively short time and only a very few tumbles she began

169

to get the feel of the ice and also to gain a little confidence, so that even Robbie, an experienced skater, was moved to offer his congratulations.

Steve looked at his watch. ' I think we'd better be going now, Fiona. Mrs Campbell said those friends of hers were coming at twelve for drinks and we promised we'd be back, didn't we?'

' Oh, *Mommy*!' Jenny's glowing face fell. ' We don't really have to go yet, do we? I'm having *such* fun! Please let me stay!'

' I'll look after her, Mrs Campbell,' Robbie said eagerly. ' She'll be all right with me. Won't you, Jenny?'

Fiona hesitated, then acquiesced. It would be unkind to make Jenny leave the ice just as she was beginning to find her rhythm, she thought, and the cold spell might not last much longer. In fact, it already seemed a little warmer: the sun on her face was quite hot.

Fiona herself was reluctant to leave the loch, not because she was anxious about Jenny, but because she didn't really feel like making polite conversation to the Campbells' guests. They were a middle-aged, rather dull couple, but at least Steve seemed to enjoy talking to them about America, which they had visited on a number of occasions. Fiona, much to her relief, was left more or less alone to sip her sherry, her mind lingering restlessly on what Tessa had told her and questing into the uncertain future.

' Lunch is nearly ready. What time did you tell Jenny to come home, Fiona?' Margaret Campbell asked, and Fiona, glancing at her watch, gave a rueful exclamation.

' One o'clock, and it's nearly half-past already! Little monkey, I expect she's enjoying herself so much

170

that she's forgotten all about the time!'

'Oh well! One is only young once,' Douglas Campbell observed. Then, his brows drawing together in a slight frown, 'Actually I'm rather surprised that the ice is strong enough for skating. We usually need a much longer period of cold weather before the loch is really safe.'

'Oh, it seemed quite all right—' Steve began, but just at that moment the telephone rang. Mrs Campbell hurried to answer it, returning a minute or two later looking so white and shocked that with a cry Fiona leaped to her feet.

'What's the matter? Why are you looking like that?' Her voice was sharp with apprehension.

'Fiona, I'm—I'm afraid it's Jenny. She—she skated too near the trees, where the ice was thinner than anyone thought, and it . . . cracked—No, it's all right!' as Fiona, ashen, swayed and nearly fell. 'They got her out, or at least Rowan did. He was passing by in his car when he heard the children screaming, and arrived in the nick of time, apparently. It was Tessa MacGregor who telephoned: she asked me to tell you that Jenny is safe and sound and that Rowan will be bringing her home in a few minutes' time.'

Fiona's face was stricken. 'Where is she now?'

'At the MacGregors' cottage. They've wrapped her up in blankets and given her brandy and hot water bottles. She—she was unconscious when Rowan pulled her out, Fiona. He saved her life, my dear.'

'He saved her life. . . .' A great flood of gratitude flooded Fiona's frightened heart. She said in a choked voice, 'Oh, thank God!' and turned blindly to Steve. She was shaking all over and he put his arm round her instinctively. She clung to him, but though he held her closely he knew with bitter certainty that the

171

support of a table or a chair would have meant no less to her. The moment that Rowan arrived with a small, blanket-wrapped figure in his arms she forgot about him altogether. He might, he thought bitterly, have become completely non-existent. She had eyes only for her daughter, and for the tall, unsmiling man whose presence of mind had saved her daughter's life.

Although at first Jenny appeared to be none the worse for her alarming experience, by the next day she had developed a feverish cold which became so much worse by nightfall that Fiona, who had spent all day at the child's bedside, was forced to send for Rowan.

He came immediately. Fiona, who had already tried with a conspicuous lack of success to thank him for what he had done—he had cut short her stammered sentences rather brusquely—looked anxiously at his brown face as he examined his small patient. Her temperature had risen and Margaret Campbell, shaking her head, had spoken of the possibility of pneumonia.

'I've got a dreadful headache.' Jenny, ill though she was, tried hard to summon a smile. 'Can you make it go away, please, Uncle Rowan?'

'I expect I can.' Rowan's voice was cheerfully reassuring, but he was frowning slightly when he emerged from the sickroom and Fiona felt her heart slam painfully against her ribs.

'Rowan, is she—is she going to be seriously ill?' In spite of herself her lips quivered.

'My dear, of course not!' Rowan's voice changed as he looked at her. He took her hands in his, firmly and quietly and with infinite friendliness and tenderness. 'She's certainly got a very nasty cold and a rather

172

high temperature, but the antibiotic I'm going to give her should arrest the infection within the next three days. She's going to be all right, I promise you that.'

Somehow Fiona believed him. She gave a long shuddering sigh. She knew she shouldn't say it, but she did.

'Oh, Rowan, how—how *glad* I am that you're here!' She tried to muster a smile, but suddenly the kindness she saw in his eyes was too much for her self-control. A sob rose in her throat and though she tried desperately to stifle it she didn't quite succeed. The next thing she knew was that Rowan's arms were round her and she was crying all over his clean white shirt. She cried for so many things and for so many people— Jenny and Steve and Tessa and Rowan himself—and all the time he held her, stroking her hair and saying nothing at all.

Neither of them saw Steve, who stood watching them for a few seconds and who then disappeared as quietly as he had come. It was the sound of a car door slamming that brought Fiona to a stunned realisation of where she was and what she was doing.

Her cheeks scarlet, she tried to pull away. 'Rowan, I—I'm terribly sorry! Why didn't you stop me? If all distraught mothers made a habit of crying on your shoulder—'

Rowan gave her an odd little smile. 'Silly girl. That's what shoulders are for, didn't you know?' he said softly. Then, producing a clean white handkerchief and drying her cheeks in a businesslike way, 'Feeling better?'

'Yes, thank you. Much. Rowan—'

'Yes, Fiona?'

She said unsteadily, 'I—I haven't thanked you properly for saving Jenny's life. You wouldn't let me.

I—I still don't know what to say—'

'You don't have to say anything.' Rowan looked down at her, his smile twisted. 'Don't you know yet that I love Jenny, too?'

He turned and left her. For a moment Fiona stood irresolute, longing to call him back, but before she could make up her mind to do so a crash from Jenny's bedroom decided the matter for her. When she investigated she found that Jenny had knocked over a glassful of water and by the time she had mopped up the mess Rowan had left the house.

As predicted, Jenny was slightly better the following morning. Rowan came to see her shortly after nine o'clock and seemed satisfied with her progress, though Fiona had no opportunity to speak to him alone.

Judi, enjoying a morning off because John Paterson was spending the day with his publishers, volunteered to entertain Steve, who, according to her, was looking 'terribly at a loose end'.

'Good thing he's going back tomorrow,' she remarked as Fiona thanked her. 'Men are horribly in the way when anyone's ill, aren't they? I mean, it's all right when they're the patients, but they do so seem to hate it when they don't happen to be the centre of attention!'

Fiona gave a rueful laugh. 'Poor Steve! I'm afraid he hasn't had a very successful trip.'

'No.' Judi wandered over to the window and stood looking out. 'There's someone coming to the house. It's a girl, I think. Gosh, what gorgeous hair!'

Fiona joined her at the window. She recognised the slender, graceful figure in the navy blue trews and anorak and smiled and waved.

'It's Tessa MacGregor. She rang up to say she'd bring back Jenny's clothes—' she began, but broke off as Judi gave a startled exclamation.

'Good heavens! It's the girl that Neil used to be so crazy about! She hasn't changed a scrap!'

Fiona felt the blood drain out of her face. She stared incredulously at Judi, who was looking as though she wished that the earth would open up and swallow her.

'What did you say?' she asked huskily and then, as Judi did not answer, 'What did you mean—it's the girl Neil used to be so crazy about? Tell me! Oh, Judi, please tell me!'

CHAPTER XI

Judi's dark-fringed eyes were wide and frightened.

'Fiona, there's nothing very much to tell! Really there isn't! And it all happened so long ago, before you and Neil were married, of course—'

'Tell me!' Fiona said again, and she herself was surprised at the inflexibility of her voice.

Judi turned away from the window. 'I never meant to say anything,' she said brokenly, her eyes anywhere but on Fiona's face. 'I know how much you loved Neil and I didn't want to hurt you. He's dead and you need never have known—'

'Known *what*?'

Judi moistened her lips. 'That—that just before he became engaged to you he was having an affair with that girl. The—the one you called Tessa MacGregor. I never knew her name before.'

Fiona was white to the lips. Her brain whirled in sick misery. 'Judi, are you sure? How—how can you possibly know? Nobody else ever did—'

'I—I didn't *spy* on them, Fiona! Please don't think that. But—but I was often at a loose end those hols, and—and I saw them together sometimes. In secret places. People don't always notice a kid hanging about and—and I'd learned to keep well out of Neil's way, anyhow. He didn't like me terribly much, as you probably remember.'

Fiona said in a hard dry voice, 'Let's get this quite straight, Judi. You—you say that you often saw Neil and Tessa together. Are you sure that—well, that they weren't just perfectly innocent meetings?'

('I hardly know the girl myself,' Neil had said when

176

telling Fiona that he had known of Rowan's attachment for Tessa. 'I don't suppose I've spoken more than half a dozen words to her in the whole of my life.')

Judi shook her head miserably. Then, as she saw Fiona's anguished expression she said with a kind of desperation, 'Oh, Fiona, please, *please* don't look like that! I feel so awful! Can't you possibly forget what I said? After all, it can hardly matter now, surely? One can't put back the clock—'

Fiona brushed her hand across her eyes. 'I'm sorry. Don't upset yourself, Judi. It—it's just been such a shock. It—I—you see, I didn't think there'd ever been anyone. Neil said—' She stopped, unable to go on.

'That you were the only girl he'd ever loved? But that's why I told you he wasn't straight, Fiona!' Judi said quickly. 'I *knew* he couldn't possibly have told you about that other girl. I—I honestly thought he was madly in love with her. It was a terrific shock when he suddenly announced his engagement to you. I—I couldn't really believe it. I—well, I did wonder whether I should say something, but I was just a kid at the time and—and I suppose I was a bit scared of landing myself in trouble.'

She paused nervously. '*Ought* I to have said anything, Fiona? I mean, would it have made much difference? Would you still have married Neil, just the same?'

Oh, Judi, Fiona thought sadly, it would have made all the difference in the world. . . . Aloud she said huskily, knowing that in this instance a kind lie was better than the truth, 'I—I expect so.'

Judi heaved a sigh of relief and her face brightened. 'Oh, *good*! Then everything's really quite all right, isn't it? You and Neil were happy together for as long as your marriage lasted and—and even if Tessa was a bit upset at being thrown over in favour of you I expect she got over her disappointment quite quickly, don't you? She's such a pretty girl, I don't suppose she's ever been short of admirers! I've even heard that our estimable Doctor Macrae is quite smitten! Have you?'

Judi obviously knew nothing at all about Tessa's baby and the anguish the girl must have undergone. It was perhaps a good thing that she didn't realise the full extent of Neil's perfidy, Fiona thought. She was saved from replying by the appearance of Margaret Campbell, who was carrying a neat brown paper parcel under her arm.

'Tessa MacGregor has just brought back Jenny's clothes, Fiona. I asked her in, but she was in a hurry and wouldn't stop. I expect you'll see her to thank her later, dear. She's washed and ironed every single thing that Jenny was wearing: wasn't it kind of her? She says that Robbie is terribly upset by what happened. He feels that Jenny was left in his charge and that you must think that he let you down very badly.'

'Oh, but that's absurd!' Fiona exclaimed. 'The accident might have happened even if I'd been there!'

'That's just what I told Tessa,' Margaret agreed.

Fiona looked at her, quiet, kind and morally upright, and her eyes blurred with sudden tears. How could such *good* people as she and Douglas have had a son like Neil? Even now she could hardly believe what Judi had told her, its implications were so utterly shattering. Neil and Tessa. Not Tessa and Rowan. . . .

She felt almost numb with shock, but later the numbness wore off and she was left the prey of deeply

178

conflicting emotions that were such a chaotic mixture of anger, humiliation, regret and searing despair that she did not think she would ever be able to disentangle them.

If Judi was right—and her words had certainly borne the chill of absolute conviction—then Neil had deceived her and lied to her. He had let her believe that it was Rowan who had been having an affair with Tessa, that it was Rowan who was the father of her unborn child. Knowing how much she, Fiona, loved him, he had deliberately blackened his friend's name. Had tricked her, ruthlessly and cold-bloodedly, into marrying him.

No wonder, Fiona thought bleakly, that despite all her efforts to make it otherwise their marriage had been such an unhappy one. How could it have been otherwise when it had been founded on a tissue of lies? So much of Neil's behaviour was now explained. He must have been tortured by feelings of guilt!

She buried her head in her arms. Neil had deceived her all the way along. His soft, spoken words had been a distortion of the truth, his kisses a betrayal, her own tears completely unnecessary. She had exiled herself from her home and from the man she loved simply because for some unaccountable reason Neil had seized his chance to do that man an irreparable wrong. . . .

Not that she herself was without blame. Fiona realised that now. She should have choked back her pride and gone to Rowan and asked him pointblank the meaning of the scene she had witnessed by the shores of the loch. Even now she didn't completely understand what had happened but there must be an answer to her rioting questions. There *must* be . . . but would she, now, ever know it? Wasn't it eight years too late to ask for an explanation . . . too late to say how sorry she was for the conclusions she'd jumped to?

She bit her quivering lips. There was still so much that baffled her. Why, on that wet and windy day at Rivendell, hadn't Rowan denied her angry accusations? Why had he let her go on believing that he had, in fact, been Tessa's lover? Was it possible that he had known quite well that Neil had been responsible for the girl's plight and that he had shouldered the blame merely to save her, Fiona, from distress and disillusionment? After all, she had been very careful to keep the truth about her unhappy marriage to herself. Like Judi, Rowan must believe that she had loved Neil very much. She had quite deliberately *made* him believe that. To save her pride. . . .

She rose and went to stand by the window. She pulled back the curtains and stared out into the darkness with pain-filled eyes. Winter had the landscape in its iron grip and the white desolation in front of her matched the desolation in her heart. There was just one difference. Spring, one day, would come to Inveray.

From far away came the melancholy sound of an owl. Then, a few minutes later, a clock chimed the hour and with a sigh Fiona roused herself. Time to give Jenny another dose of her antibiotic.

At any rate, she thought, she still had Jenny. Thanks to Rowan. Some good, at least, had come out of her disastrous marriage. But oh, if only Jenny had been Rowan's daughter!

Steve left Inveray the next day. He kissed Fiona good-bye, but without passion. In fact, his lips merely brushed her brow.

' God bless, Fiona,' he said quietly.

She had been so preoccupied with Jenny that she

had scarcely had time to notice the change in his attitude towards her. Now, however, she realised that he was saying goodbye to her as a friend rather than as a dissatisfied lover and she looked at him with puzzled eyes.

'Steve, I'm—I'm sorry things have turned out the way they have. I—I do like you so enormously. I hope that when Jenny and I come back to America we can still go on being friends?'

He looked at her oddly. 'You are planning to come back, then?'

'Of course.' She made answer lightly. 'Very soon, I expect—directly Jenny is really fit again, in fact. I shall have to write to Lissa and ask her to start airing our beds!'

Steve gave her a whimsical little smile. 'Oh, Fiona! Wouldn't it be far more sensible to stay where your heart is?' Then, as she stared at him blankly, he took hold of her hand. 'I know how you feel about Macrae, my dear. You love him, don't you? That's really why you've refused to marry me.'

Fiona felt her heart slip into a hurried beat. For a moment she was tempted to utter a denial, but almost immediately she put the temptation from her. If she owed Steve anything at all for his faithful friendship over the past few years, she owed him truth and nothing but the truth.

'Yes, Steve, I do. But—but there isn't any future in it. There's someone else, you see.'

Tessa . . . it must be Tessa. The whole clachan was buzzing with excited rumours. Tessa was wearing a beautiful sapphire ring on her engagement finger and though she laughed and blushed and refused to say anything when she was challenged by curious friends and neighbours everyone was busy linking her name with Rowan's. He was, after all, a frequent caller at the MacGregors' cottage. There'd been no one else. Well, good luck to her, Fiona thought. She deserved any happiness that was now coming her way.

Steve frowned, thinking of the expression that he had seen on Rowan's face when he had held Fiona in his arms and let her cry on his shoulder. It was that incident that had made him realise that he must say goodbye for ever to his hope of making Fiona his wife.

' Are you sure?'

' Quite sure,' Fiona answered him steadily.

Steve seemed to accept her statement, for he said quietly, ' I'm very sorry. If I can't have you myself, my dear—and I've accepted the fact that I can't, so don't worry about it—I'd like to see you married to a man like Macrae. You mean a great deal to me, you know, and there's nothing I'd like better than to see you really happy. Jenny too.'

' Oh, *Steve*!' Fiona swallowed a sob as she watched him depart, and Judi, coming unexpectedly into the room, found her dabbing at her eyes.

' Tears, Fiona?' she asked, raising her brows. ' You must be rather fonder of your American friend than you've given anyone reason to suspect!'

In spite of herself Fiona gave a choked little laugh. ' He's such a dear! I don't want to marry him one little bit, but I do like him and I know I shall miss him.'

' Well, cheer up! I've got some interesting news for you,' Judi said, perching herself on the arm of a chair. ' Bruce wants to marry me and I think I probably will. Not immediately, perhaps, but at some time in the not too distant future!'

' Judi!'

Judi grinned. ' I told you I'd come to Inveray to

find a husband! I thought it was going to be Rowan, but I'm really quite glad that he'd have none of me! I've come to the conclusion that I'd much rather have dear old Bruce!'

'Words fail me!' Fiona said helplessly.

'I thought you might be surprised,' Judi said smugly. 'I'm quite surprised myself, come to that. Do you know, I'm even resigned to spending the rest of my life in Inveray?' She shook her head with mock sadness. 'There's no doubt about it. I've been debauched—or do I mean demoralised? Which means something awful?'

She was talking nonsense, Fiona suddenly realised, to disguise the fact that for perhaps the first time in her life she was shy and unsure of herself. It was a good sign!

She said warmly, 'Judi! Don't try to pull the wool over my eyes! I believe you're head over heels in love with Bruce Buchanan and have been all along, even when you were making eyes at Rowan!'

'That's what I think, too!' Judi admitted. Then, with a laugh, 'Do I look any different? I feel just as though I've got a neon sign fixed round my neck with "I love Bruce" written on it in letters a foot high!'

Certainly the news of her engagement to Bruce became very quickly known.

'Well, I hear best wishes and congratulations are very much in order!' Rowan, paying an evening visit to Jenny to check on her progress, stayed for a glass of sherry afterwards and greeted Judi with a teasing smile. 'I hope poor Buchanan knows how much trouble he's laying up for himself? He's a braver man than I could ever hope to be and that's a fact!'

'Don't we know it! Pig!' Judi hurled a cushion at him which he caught and returned to Margaret

Campbell with a little bow.

'Engagements seem to be in the air,' she observed with a smile. 'I heard today that Tessa MacGregor is getting married in April. She's been wearing an engagement ring for several days, but apparently she didn't want to make any official announcement until her fiancé could join her here in Inveray. I hear he's a Glaswegian and a one-time colleague of yours, Rowan?'

'Yes—Alec Shaw. He was at medical college with me,' Rowan told her. 'I've known about their friendship for a very long time and I'm extremely happy about it.'

Fiona, feeling like someone waking up from a bad dream, heard Judi say laughingly, 'I suppose you realise that half the clachan has been tipping you as the lucky man, Rowan? What a disappointment to find that you're heartwhole and fancy free after all!'

'I wouldn't say that. But as for Tessa—yes, I did know that our names were being linked together, but though it rather worried her I thought the gossips might as well have a field day. Being proved wrong may teach a few of them to keep a still tongue in their heads in future,' Rowan said laconically.

Margaret Campbell, struck by Fiona's sudden pallor, looked at her anxiously. 'My dear, do you feel all right? You look terribly pale. Are you faint?'

Fiona, feeling Rowan's eyes upon her, rose hurriedly to her feet. 'No, I'm quite all right, thanks. But—but if you'll excuse me I'll just go and see if Jenny's asleep.'

She was. Fiona had known quite well that she would be. Jenny's cheeks were flushed and her eyelashes lay on them like curled golden fans. In one small outstretched hand she clutched a tiny dressed doll that Rowan had brought her that evening.

Gently Fiona disengaged the small fingers and placed the doll on Jenny's bedside table. It would almost certainly be the first thing she looked for in the morning, not so much because she liked dolls but because Rowan had given it to her.

He was not going to marry Tessa! As she straightened Jenny's blankets Fiona was aware of a fierce joy that although there was to be a happy ending to Tessa's story, Rowan himself was not going to supply it.

She thought of Neil, who had been responsible for so much heartache, and drew a long quivering breath. Surely if anyone deserved a second chance it was Tessa! A second chance . . . wasn't it what she herself longed for? The chance to tell Rowan that she was sorry, to wipe out the heartbreak of the last eight years, to pull down the barriers that existed between them.

She left Jenny's bedroom and passed into her own. Neil's photograph smiled at her from the dressing table. She picked it up and stared at it wonderingly. Why had he acted as he had? Why had he been so cruel? There was nothing in his handsome face to suggest that he was capable of treachery and deceit. He looked what most people had always believed him to be—a gay, good-natured young man.

'Oh, Neil!' Fiona whispered, and put back the photograph with fingers that trembled in spite of herself. Then she switched off the light and went slowly downstairs, dragging her feet a little because she suddenly felt bone-weary. Her head ached and she was conscious of an overpowering urge to escape from the confines of the house.

The moon was nearly full when she went out and in its pale, frosty light the garden was a place of wonder, with the bare trees casting fairy-like traceries upon the white carpet spread out beneath them.

It was very cold. Fiona buttoned her coat up around her throat and as she did so a voice behind her said, 'I thought I heard you go out. Why the sudden desire for solitude, Fiona?'

Rowan! Her heart thumping, she swung round to find him standing behind her with his hands in his coat pockets, eyeing her sardonically. In the moonlight his face seemed dark and almost satyr-like.

She said breathlessly, 'I—I just wanted a breath of fresh air. I—I haven't been outside the house at all since Jenny became ill.' Then, brightly, 'She's a lot better, isn't she, Rowan? She says she'd like to get up tomorrow. Do you think she can?'

'We'll talk about Jenny later. Right now I want to talk about you.'

'M-me?'

'Yes. You looked very odd when your mother-in-law and I were talking about Tessa. Tell me, Fiona, were you disappointed to find that the rumours were incorrect? Did you think that in the interests of justice it was I who should make an honest woman of Tessa MacGregor, if I may use so outdated a phrase?'

She had heard that raw bitterness in his voice before and now she knew the reason for it. She winced.

In a scarcely audible voice she said, 'No.'

'Really? You do surprise me.'

Her heart twisted with pain at the mockery she saw in his eyes, and she drew a deep breath.

'Rowan, there's—there's something I want to tell you. In fact, I must tell you. I—I know about Neil and Tessa. I know that he was the father of her child, not you.'

The silence stretched. For what seemed an eternity

186

Fiona did not dare to look at the man who stood beside her, and when at last she did so his face was lost in shadow, so that she could not see his expression.

'Who told you?' His voice, incredibly, held something that might have been anger. 'Not Tessa? She promised me—' He stopped abruptly.

'No, it wasn't Tessa. It was Judi. She saw Tessa when she came to the house the other evening and recognised her. Apparently she'd seen her and Neil together, years ago.' She swallowed. 'Rowan, why did you let me think that it was you who treated Tessa so badly? Why didn't you tell me the truth? You knew it . . . you've always known it, haven't you?'

'Yes, I have. But apart from anything else, if I'd told you the truth would you have believed me, Fiona? Loving Neil the way you did—'

'No!' The word was wrung from her lips almost against her will. 'No, this time you're wrong! I didn't love him! I never did!'

Rowan stared at her. 'You didn't love him?' His voice was incredulous. 'But you must have done! You ditched me without a qualm in order to marry him—you accepted without any sort of verification the story he later told you about Tessa and myself—'

Fiona's eyes met his, wildly. 'Rowan, I lied to you about that. I acted as I did because of Tessa! You see, I—I saw you with her, by the loch. I heard her beg you for help! I was heartbroken and bewildered. I—I didn't know what to do, whom to turn to.' She swallowed a sob as she heard Rowan suck in his breath, and hurried on. 'Neil found me crying. I asked him if it was true that you and Tessa were having an affair. He said yes, it was, that he'd known about it for months. He—he knew about the baby as well. He said you'd told him. And—and he said that if I married him you'd probably do the right thing by Tessa.'

Rowan caught hold of her, his hands gripping her arms. 'My God! Neil did . . . *that*?' There was horror and incredulity in his voice.

Fiona's eyes filled with tears. 'Yes. Why, Rowan? Why would he have wanted to do such a terrible thing?'

There was another silence. Then very slowly, his face sombre, Rowan said, 'Fiona, if you really never loved Neil then I can speak frankly, without worrying about spoiling your illusions. Neil was a liar, and a born opportunist. He made trouble for me several times at school. I came to suspect that he had hated and resented me all through the years that he had professed friendship for me, though he managed to hide his feelings so successfully that I was never really sure.' He stopped, then added bitterly, 'He was about the only person who knew how much I loved you. When he realised that you'd jumped to the wrong conclusions about Tessa and myself I think he saw a heaven-sent chance to knock me off my seat in the clouds and send me crashing to the ground. I think it's likely that his mind was so warped and twisted that he regarded it as a kind of fitting revenge.'

Fiona caught her breath. 'You're probably right.' She told him, then, about the diary she had found among Neil's possessions.

Rowan nodded. 'Yes, that fits.' He paused, then added in a different voice, 'But how on earth you could have believed that I'd been having an affair with Tessa after all I'd said to you—'

'Rowan, I didn't want to believe it! I didn't!' The colour left Fiona's cheeks: her heart felt cold with regret as she realised what Rowan must think of her.

'It was just that I didn't understand. Why did Tessa appeal to you for help? Why you, and not Neil?'

'She knew she'd get no help from Neil. It was when he heard about the baby that he suddenly decided to emigrate. He told her that she'd got no proof that he was the child's father and that if she tried to do anything about it he would deny all responsibility. It was then that she came to me. She thought that as a doctor I might be able to help her. Of course I couldn't.'

He paused. 'I'd had my suspicions, but it wasn't until after the baby died that I knew for certain that Neil was the father. By that time you and Neil were married and I'd heard from the Campbells that you were expecting a child yourself.' He drew a deep breath. 'I made Tessa promise that she would never do or say anything that might spoil your . . . happiness. In return, Father and I helped her, financially and in other ways. I'm glad we did. She's a fine girl—too fine to be ruined by a man like Neil Campbell!'

Fiona caught her breath. 'She . . . must have loved him very much.'

'I think she did. She was very young and innocent at the time.' He sighed. 'Alec knows her whole story and I think it's made him love her more, not less. Courage is something that he rates very highly and it's something that Tessa has in abundance. She's not only had to get over Neil's betrayal, poor girl, but the baby's death as well. It was a little girl, and she adored her.'

Fiona shut her eyes, remembering the expression of yearning sadness on Tessa's face the day that she and Jenny had called at the MacGregors' cottage to see Robbie's hamster. Huskily she said, 'I hope she'll be happy now, Rowan.'

'I think she will. In fact, I'm sure she will.' He

189

paused, and his voice changed, became light and cool. 'You'll be happy, too, won't you, with Steve Connaught? All's well that ends well, to quote the immortal bard.'

'I'm not going to marry Steve.' Fiona spoke steadily. He stared at her. 'You're not? But I thought—'

Fiona was trembling. This time, she thought, she would not let her courage fail her. This time she would humble her pride and listen to what her heart told her to say.

Quietly she said, 'I married Neil as a means of escape. I married him and I never stopped loving you. Do you imagine that I haven't learned my lesson? That I'd be stupid enough to make the same mistake again?

In his eyes she saw a dawning wonder. 'Fiona! You don't mean—you can't mean—'

'I mean that I love you,' she said softly. 'Always and always and always. Even when I fought against it most. It's been you all the time—'

She got no further, for Rowan caught her in his arms and kissed her with a passion and tenderness that sent the blood singing in her veins.

'Oh, Fiona!' he said huskily, when at last he raised his head. 'I've never forgotten you, please believe that. Directly I saw you again I knew, too, that despite all the disappointment and bitterness of losing you to Neil I still loved you, still wanted you. I thought that perhaps there might be a chance for me, but you were so cold and distant—and then I heard about Connaught from Jenny—'

Fiona clung to him. 'You didn't know that there was a barrier of lies between us. Perhaps if Duncan MacGregor hadn't become ill and Tessa hadn't returned to Inveray, we might never have known what a false barrier it was.' She shivered. 'Oh, Rowan, it doesn't bear thinking about!'

'Then don't think about it, my darling. Think about the future instead—*our* future. Yours and Jenny's and mine. You know I'd not planned to stay in Inveray? Father can do without me now.' He looked at her a little anxiously. 'Is that a disappointment?'

'Not to me. I'll be happy wherever you are, Rowan.'

Rowan laughed. 'At any rate we'll stay in Scotland. That will please Jenny, won't it?'

'And her grandparents! They've been dreading our return to America,' Fiona said, knowing, as she spoke, that the Campbells would be overjoyed at the news that she and Rowan were to be married. Since they had lost Neil they had come to look on Rowan almost as a second son.

Rowan's arms were like a band of steel around her, but his eyes were very tender as he kissed her. 'What are you thinking about my darling?'

'About the eight years we've wasted. I wish we could have them back, Rowan.'

Rowan tipped up her chin and said softly, 'No regrets, Fiona. Do you know that poem by Elizabeth Jennings?' Then, as she shook her head, he quoted softly

'" Let us have winter loving that the heart
    May be in peace and ready to partake
    Of the slow pleasure spring would wish to hurry
    Or that in summer harshly would awake. . . ." '

Winter loving. . . . Fiona closed her eyes. Yes, it sounded good. She looked at Rowan and smiled. All wistfulness vanished as she lifted her face to his and said contentedly, 'You're right. Winter loving will do for me.'

'And for me,' said Rowan, and bent to take her lips.

Why the smile?

... because she has just received her **Free Harlequin Romance Catalogue!**

... and now she has a complete listing of the many, many Harlequin Romances still available.

... and now she can pick out titles by her favorite authors or fill in missing numbers for her library.

You too may have a **Free Harlequin Romance Catalogue** (and a smile!), simply by mailing in the coupon below.